STOLEN
by the
LAIRD

By
Eliza Knight

She was supposed to be his prize... But not all rewards are sweet...

Laird Brody Keith, Marischal of Scotland, has been asked by his future king to travel with William Wallace to Dunnottar Castle, where they will seize the castle back from the English. If he completes his mission, the castle, the land and all it holds, will be his. Brody is more than eager to sink his blade into the hearts of his enemies after the brutal murder of his sister and father. But what he doesn't count on is finding an English lass in need of his protection...

Lady Guinevere has led a less than pleasant life in Scotland over the past year, and now she can either run for her life or accept the proposal of a man who should be her enemy. Survival bids her to acquiesce, but that doesn't mean she has to play nice. Except, she's coming to adore the people whom she's always been told she should hate, and respect the man who risked his life for her.

Joined for a mutual purpose, Brody and Guinevere seem doomed from the start, but as time passes and their true enemies draw closer, they'll form an alliance that not even the devil himself can break.

DEDICATION

For you, dear reader. Thank you for reading my stories!

Dear Reader,

In 1297, William Wallace led a siege on the castle, capturing 4000 English and burning them in the church alive. Dunnottar Castle was not granted to the Earls of Marischal/Clan Keith until much later in the 14th century, but for the purpose of this story, I have moved that date up.

Here is part of a poem written about the event…

Therefore a fire was brought speedily:
Which burnt the church, and all those South'ron boys:
Out o'er the rock the rest rush'd great noise;
Some hung on craigs, and loath were to die.
Some lap, some fell, some flutter'd in the sea;
And perish'd all, not one remain'd alive.
Extract of Blind Harry 'Wallace' c1470s

I do hope you enjoy this story!

Best wishes and happy reading,

Eliza

Eliza Knight

CHAPTER ONE

Scottish Highlands
October, 1297

"Your future awaits." William Wallace, the Guardian of Scotland, smiled with glee, the brightness in his eyes bordering on maniacal.

Chief Brody Keith, Marischal of Scotland, returned the warlord's grin, though his own was much more subdued. "I'm honored to be given such a reward from our future king."

"Indeed. He is pleased with your service, as am I. Dunnottar and all it holds will soon be yours."

All it held at present was a bunch of rotten Sassenachs, a reward not so sweet. Brody nodded grimly. He hated the English with a passion, but the one thing he loathed more than their blackened souls was what they were doing to his country and his people.

Brody was willing to cross any path, no matter how dangerous, to exterminate the vermin that had inhabited their lands. This journey was proving to be just that.

Surrounded on three sides by ocean, cliffs and gullies, the terrain to Dunnottar Castle was treacherous. More than once, a horse in the massive war camp's caravan had slipped, causing injury and near death to several. There was also the unfortunate reality that the road to the castle allowed plenty of places to be spotted by one's enemy.

With the onset of nightfall and clouds filtering over the moon, they had little way of seeing the path and were forced to make camp.

This did not bode well.

Brody had accompanied William Wallace and their armies comprised of six-thousand strong, on the orders of his soon-to-be king, Robert de Brus, to take back Dunnottar Castle from the bloody English who'd massacred the men of God that once inhabited the place.

The previous year, the bloody Sassenachs had sailed in on ships, thousands strong, and taken control of the castle and its village. The villagers were forced to run or bend to the will of the English. They were no match for the mass of English force and there'd been no time to call in reinforcements—until now.

Dunnottar had been a place of religious use and the damned English had run the men of God off. Those who'd stayed in the castle's defense were quickly murdered. If that wasn't saying they were dealing with the devil's disciples, Brody wasn't sure what would.

He climbed down from his horse, Thunder, rubbing the massive black warhorse's neck and whispering his thanks. Thunder snorted, nudging Brody in the shoulder. After leading his mount to water and seeing that he had a bucket of oats as a prize for his good work, Brody made his way toward one of the campfires in search of sustenance and whisky.

"Marischal." Wallace sat down beside him on the ground, passing him a leg of overcooked fowl.

Brody took a bite, and rather than grimacing at the burnt rubbery taste, he swallowed it down with gratitude that he had anything to eat at all.

"I have a plan, though it may be mad," Wallace mused.

By now, Brody should have been used to Wallace's plans, having been with him most recently at the Battle of Stirling Bridge. Alas, anything unplanned, or even mildly mad, made Brody a little nervous. He was a warrior of action, aye, but also a man who plotted strategy taking risks into consideration. Despite his own reservations, Wallace had not led them astray just yet.

"I have faith your plan will benefit Scotland." Brody took another large bite of leathered meat, swallowing it down with a great gulp of ale passed to him by his cousin and second in command, Noah.

Wallace chuckled. "Think ye there'll be a pretty wench awaiting ye?"

Brody grimaced. De Brus had written an edict that Brody had rolled and tucked up his sleeve. Dunnottar and the lands were to fall under his jurisdiction. All he had to do was take it back from the English. Their future king had alluded that should he wish to take a bride, now would be a good time, but Brody had brushed away that comment. He wasn't certain he ever wanted to wed. Aye, as a chief and laird, 'twas his duty to carry on his line. But, truth be told, he was so embroiled in the war with the English, he wasn't certain he'd live long enough to see a bairn or spend enough time in his wife's bed to see one created.

Brody swished ale around his mouth, trying to get the burnt taste out. "I've no use for a bride just yet. What is your plan?"

The first of several raindrops fell on his face. He gave it five minutes before the heavens opened in earnest. They were lucky with Beltane's impending approach to have a mild night despite the rain. It wasn't unheard of to already have frost come morning at this time of year.

"We will attack tonight," Wallace said. "They will not be expecting it with the dark and now the rain. The English run and hide when it rains, as though a few drops might melt them."

"Perhaps it does." Brody chuckled. "They wouldna be expecting us, but what about the terrain? 'Twas dangerous to traverse dry, will be doubly treacherous wet. 'Tis why we had the men make camp."

"Aye. But come morning, the guards at Dunnottar will see us and fire upon us."

Brody snatched a stale bannock from a basket being passed, breaking it in half and handing a piece to Wallace. "So we must choose the lesser of two evils."

Wallace bit into the bannock, crumbs gathering in his beard. "Aye. And we must climb."

Brody raised a brow at Wallace's outrageous suggestion. "Traversing the narrow passage to get to the gate is one thing, but asking the men to climb in the dark, that is quite another."

"Nay, nay, ye misunderstand me, Marischal, 'twill just be ye and me doing the climbing. We'll scale the cliff and creep toward the top of the tower where it meets. We'll dispatch the guard there and open the portcullis to the men."

Brody grunted. He was a good rock climber and so was Wallace. After the Battle of Stirling Bridge, when they'd crossed into the Grampian Mountains, the two of them had an ongoing wager about who could climb the fastest. Every cliffside they passed, they stopped to race to the top, the men cheering them on. The stakes rose with each additional climb until Brody allowed the new Guardian to win at de Brus' urging.

While he hated to forfeit, Brody could see why it was important for the men to think Wallace was unbeatable. They needed to believe they were following the best man. And they were. No one else had Wallace's drive, save for his cousin, Moray.

"I think we can manage," Brody said. Aye, the plan was mad, but between the two of them, they could see it done. Besides, Brody loved a challenge.

"Good. Let's tell the men. Finish up that goose and we'll leave."

Brody managed to choke down the rest of his charred meat, tossing the bone to one of the war dogs in their camp.

He took a swig of whisky and then stood, stretching out his spine, cracking his neck and fingers. To Noah, he said, "Ye know what to do should I fall and break my neck."

"Marry your wee sister off to the lowest man in the clan and take your position as Marischal?" Noah winked. Since childhood, they'd made the running joke that with only sisters second in line, should Brody die, Noah would attempt anything to seize power. But a joke it was, for Noah was the most loyal of men, and with his betrothal to the Oliphant Clan lass, he was due to inherit quite a bit of land through marriage.

"As long as the man isn't Blind Harry, then I'm certain Maire will be most pleased." Blind Harry had to be over one hundred years old. He was the oldest man in the Keith Clan and he'd been around as long as anyone could remember. He'd been blinded by the enemy before Brody was born. But Brody could swear the man could see given the number of times he'd caught them misbehaving as children.

Noah reached up and Brody took hold of his arm, hoisting him up.

"In all honesty, cousin, I will look after her and be certain she marries a man who will carry on your legacy with ye in mind. I will look after everyone. Ye can trust me."

"I know it, Noah." Brody grinned and slapped his cousin on the back. "But we need not worry. I shall see ye on the other side of that tower. I will not let a little thing like death stop me from beating Wallace at a climb."

"I have no doubt."

With one final, masculine embrace, Brody approached William Wallace.

"Are ye ready, Guardian?"

Wallace grinned, that maniacal smile, shadows from the campfires bouncing on his bearded face. "Want to put a wager on it? Our morning rations?"

"Aye." No warrior wanted to go hungry. And especially not after a battle they'd be fighting tonight.

Wallace turned to the men. "Be ready to storm the entrance, even if we're only able to get the portcullis up a quarter of the way. With only the two us against a rumored English garrison of four thousand, we're going to need all the help we can get."

"Aye," the men said in unison.

"After ye," Wallace said, his tone a might too jovial for what they were about to undertake.

With the men preparing to leave camp in a line behind them, Brody and Wallace crouched low, keeping close to the one hundred sixty foot tall cliff. The rock-strewn ground beneath their boots was growing slicker with the increasing rain—which only meant the rocky crag upon which they were about to climb to reach the top of the tower would also be slippery, made more so by mossy growths.

They were two miles from the front gate. There were only two other entrances besides the main gate. A steep stone staircase carved from the cliff down near the beach—one hundred sixty steps in all and visible from the heavily guarded postern gate.

The other was an escape hatch, nearly twenty feet in the air, meant for those coming out, not going in—and it was somewhere near the top of those stairs.

The gate tower must have stood forty feet in the air, which was how high they'd have to climb to reach the top—if they weren't spotted first.

They paused when they were roughly a quarter mile away. They'd have to round a bend and if the moon was to shine in just the right way, the guards on the tower would see them clearly.

"We will need to move fast," Wallace said. "Else they spot us."

Brody squinted at the tower. "From the looks of it, there are only two guards on duty."

"Aye."

Keeping to the wall, they slid slowly another tenth of a mile, stopping to make certain they were still not seen.

The high, imposing and treacherous crag served as the walls to the fortress above. One only had to scale it—and not be seen—to lay siege to the keep beyond. No one had been brave enough to try it yet.

Before agreeing to Wallace's plan to lay siege to the northern fortress, Brody had reservations. He agreed, without a doubt, it was an important stronghold that should be under Scottish rule, but he wasn't certain it could be done. The cliff and surrounding territory were seemingly impenetrable. If they could draw the English out, they could fight them and win, but should the bastards hole up behind the solid fortress, there was little hope of getting inside without considerable losses on their part.

The English had taken it from religious men, men who would not raise a sword, but rather their hands to the heavens. And many had died. The few who escaped, including a bishop, had found de Brus and Wallace and told them of what happened.

Wallace, who'd had dealings with the English general residing there now, had needed no time to think on the matter before deciding they would lay siege.

According to historical scrolls in de Brus' possession, there had been a few successful sieges beforehand, dating back six hundred years. If their forefathers could take the castle, then perhaps there was hope they could as well.

Brody was the Marischal of Scotland after all. He was in charge of protecting the king's body and the Honours of Scotland. If his future king requested something of him, he was obligated to see it done.

Dunnottar would prove to be the best place to house the king's regalia—for when it was time to officially crown de Brus King of Scotland, Conqueror of the English. Currently, the items were placed in a locked chest hidden in an underground tunnel at Brody's castle, Keith Marischal, in East Lothian. But despite the reinforcements put into place there, dangers were still posed. Not like here at Dunnottar.

The English had ships and he'd commandeer them after taking the castle, sailing the North Sea back to East Lothian, where he could gather his family, the crown's regalia, and bring them back, rather than risking his sister's life on the rocky terrain. Brody hadn't seen any ships as they traversed the landscape, but they were likely moored on the northern shore of the castle. And once he took down the English bastards, he would claim them as his own.

After all, de Brus had said in his edict the castle, the lands, and all it held. With his already large army, adding a fleet of ships would only increase his own might and ability to protect his future king.

"Let us climb," Wallace said.

Brody nodded, tugging on his leather, iron-studded gloves. He'd had the tanner and blacksmith who traveled with them to make weapons and armor for the men create the special gloves. The iron studs were on the fingers and palms, and the leather tightened at his wrist with a small belt. Special climbing gloves. He attached the iron spikes to his boot tips and Wallace followed suit. When they'd been making sport of climbing the Grampians, Brody had gifted their Guardian with a set of each.

They crossed themselves and sent up a prayer that God would honor their lives in revenging Scottish monks and in saving their beloved country.

Brody grabbed hold of a rock overhead, testing its wetness and sturdiness. It came loose and tumbled to the ground. He swept his hands along the rock's face taking note that there were many loosened stones.

"Careful," he warned Wallace. "'Tis made of puddingstone."

Wallace let out a frustrated sound. "Ballocks, this is going to be harder than we thought."

"Check the strength before putting weight to it," Brody said, gripping on to another rock. This one felt solid.

He found a foothold and hoisted himself up. One foot down and thirty-nine to go.

Taking his time and feeling each rock before gripping it or stepping onto it, he slowly ascended the cliffside. Halfway up, he nearly lost his grip, but had a good enough hold with his other hand that he didn't fall. Wallace also had a near miss, but soon, they were both at the top, crawling forward onto the wet grass and collapsing. Brody's lungs stung from alternately holding his breath and gasping. This might have been the hardest climb of his life. In the dark. In the rain. He was damned lucky to make it. Wasn't that a sure sign that Dunnottar belonged to him?

Hearts pounding, they tucked away their gloves and boot tips, and instead pulled out their swords. They knelt upon a grassy bank. Just fifty feet away was the top of the gate tower where the men walked, seemingly oblivious to their impending death. In the torchlight, Brody made out that they wore the livery of Edward I, more appropriately named Longshanks for his long legs, which Brody wouldn't mind personally lopping off.

Though his younger sister, Maire, and his mother were alive and well at home in Keith Marischal, his older sister, Johanna, had been brutally raped and murdered by the English the year before. The Battle of Dunbar had claimed their father's life and the English, high on their victory, tried to lay siege to Keith Marischal—their intent to steal the King of Scotland's Honours and present it to Longshanks. Well, as it turned out, the only things they were able to steal were his sister and father's lives.

Brody had yet to get his hands on the man responsible. Another Sassenach general, a man named Gray, but when he did, he was going to unleash all holy hell on the bastard.

Glancing toward his friend and leader, Brody said, "Time to thrash some *Sassenach* arse."

CHAPTER TWO

Lady Guinevere sipped a cup of spiced wine by candlelight in her chamber, surrounded by her three ladies-in-waiting. They each held some clothing they were mending; shirts, nightrails, gowns, her way of giving back to the people. They sewed and mended for the people who served her husband and the castle, even though most of them despised her for being English.

The last year in Scotland had been utter hell for her. The daughter of noble English parents, she'd been married off at the young age of nineteen to an Englishman of equal standing. Baron de Ros, a knight and general in King Edward I's army, had barely waited a day before forcing her onto a ship—part of her dowry—to traverse the choppy swells of the

North Sea and lay witness to the carnage he and his men had seen done to the poor men of God upon arriving at Dunnottar.

Even though they were Scottish, she'd spent every day since praying for the souls of those departed and, begrudgingly, for that of her husband and his men.

Her husband, Baron de Ros, was a man of fortune. His king had gifted him many gold coins for having taken such an impressive holding, a place for the English to hold quarter while seizing the Highlands.

Guinevere despised de Ros.

She despised Scotland.

In fact, she despised this sickening sweet spiced wine, too.

She longed for the wine that always graced her mother's table. Her father was the Earl of Arundel. Since she was the oldest of his daughters—no sons—her husband had been promised by the king to have the title of earl on her father's passing if he were to come north. Her three younger sisters were still unmarried, living at home.

With each prick of her needle and thread through the fabric, she counted the ways in which she hated this dreaded country.

It was always cold here. The air was damp even when the sun was shining. She was isolated with no castles or English nearby. There were never any festivities, but instead much doom and gloom. They were at war and a constant fear niggled at the base of her skull. She could barely sleep because of it—and because of the cold.

Their cook, whom she suspected must have been a seamstress or some such before, was terrible at her duties because the food itself was terrible, though neatly dressed.

23

The food was so unappetizing, in fact, Guinevere had lost several inches and had to have her dresses taken in. But every time she tried to speak to Cook about various recipes she'd had at home, the woman raised up her butcher knife as though she wished to chop it right through Guinevere's throat, and so she backed out of the kitchen, returning to her room, and the undercooked chicken, or overcooked fennel.

The worst part, though, was what this place and marriage to a selfish warmongering man had done to her head.

Guinevere was not a hateful, spiteful person. She'd never been predisposed to mood swings or the like, but it seemed like ever since she'd said her wedding vows, all she could do was complain and nag and the urge to cry was incessant.

Saints, but it was horrible. This was not her. This was not her mind. And yet it was. Silently, she fought this internal battle, waiting for the day she would open her eyes, breathe in a sigh of relief, and simply be happy.

At first, her ladies had insisted she must be with child. Why else would her moods so swiftly have changed? Abigail, Claudia and Elinor had been in her household since they were girls—fostering with Guinevere's mother, the Countess of Arundel—and they knew her better than anyone else. But she was certain she was not with child. In order to be with child, one had to... do the deed.

There had certainly been enough tries on de Ros' part, but never had he actually succeeded. She wondered if it was because he'd never been with a woman before, which he'd admitted one drunken night. Or perhaps it was because he came to bed inebriated, or maybe it was her and she did not rouse him to do the deed. But after he grew frustrated one night and slapped her for it, she decided to make good use of his drunken states. She pricked her finger and smeared blood on his withered member, her thighs and a little on the sheets. That had been back at his castle in England, before they'd made the treacherous journey to Scotland. He'd not tried when they were aboard ship, for she'd been vomiting the entire crossing, and then when they'd arrived he'd been quite busy maiming and murdering. When he did find time to come to her room, she served him a cup of wine filled with herbs that helped him into sleep and the next morning she praised his prowess. The times that he'd not accepted her wine, she'd learned to perform other acts with her hands and mouth that left him satisfied and herself intact. For some reason, she held on to the fact that either he would die in battle soon, for these ferocious Scots would not let him live long, and then she could still be married high for having kept herself intact, or if she gained enough courage, she could appeal the wedding, begging for an annulment citing lack of consummation as the reasoning.

Her secret, that she was still a virgin, though wed for over a year now, she'd not even shared with her ladies. They thought the herbal wine was her own, to help her sleep given so much change had certainly caused a shock to her system.

Her ladies were to serve with her for two years and then they were each promised to return to England and whatever fates were in store for them, marriages most likely. And though Guinevere would miss them immensely, for she couldn't remember a time without them, she was also glad for them to find their own happiness. To return to a place that was not always filled with fear. And to stop having to lie to them about what she'd gone through with her wifely duties thus far—or lack of *going through*.

Elinor stood by the window, gazing out toward the gate. "It's raining again," she muttered.

"When is ever not?" Guinevere replied dryly.

"Shall I call for the fire to be stoked?"

Guinevere stood. "I can do it myself." Most of the servants were Scottish, beaten into serving her husband and his men. They were worked to the bone and given the darkness, most would likely be exhausted. She hated to work them harder than necessary. Besides, tending a fire was an easy sort of thing and she could stab at the logs pretending they were her husband.

Her legs felt heavy as she trudged toward the fire. She stared into the flames as she took hold of the poker. She prodded the burning embers, watching sparks fly, one coming dangerously close to the hem of her skirt, but she didn't even jump back. She simply watched it sizzle and pop on the wood-planked floor.

Abigail joined her, bending to put two logs crisscrossed over the charred and burning ones. Tiny sparks caught against the sides of the logs, igniting in a blaze.

Guinevere returned the poker to its holder and rubbed her hands in front of the newly brought to life flames. She covered her mouth as a yawn took over.

"Shall I help you to undress for bed?" Abigail asked.

"I suppose we should be going to bed." Though she'd yawned and her body was exhausted, she didn't truly want to sleep either.

"Did… the baron say if he was coming to visit you this evening?" Abigail asked softly.

"He did not. Judging from his disposition at dinner he is most likely snoring in the great hall." Thank goodness for small favors.

Elinor left the window to place some flat rocks by the hearth where they would heat and then be added beneath the sheets and blankets of their beds to keep them all warm at night.

Claudia poured fresh water from the basin into the pitcher for Guinevere to wash her hands and face.

Their routine rarely wavered. The only difference was if her husband was coming to visit. Instead of climbing into bed, she donned a robe over her nightrail and sat by the hearth waiting. Her ladies left the chamber to sleep in the adjoining bedchamber. If he wasn't coming, then her ladies took turns sleeping beside her. The more warm bodies together, the better.

Guinevere turned around so Abigail could begin untying her gown, when there came a single shout from outside.

"What the devil?" Guinevere murmured.

That shout was not followed by any other and had sounded rather like it was cut short. Perhaps the guards were being idiots? She wouldn't be surprised. But still, warning pins and needles were jabbing her insides. Guinevere eased her way toward the window and stared down at the bailey below.

Several men that had been sitting around a bonfire in the center of the bailey, stood and looked about them in confusion. In the quiet solitude of this treacherous mountain, they seemed quite alone. But it would appear that was not quite the case.

One of the guards on the wall shouted something that didn't quite catch on the wind.

Guinevere gazed toward the gate tower. There were two men there. Just as before. They raised their hands toward the other men, an indication that all was well.

Why then did she still feel as though something were terribly wrong?

She leaned closer toward the window, squinting her eyes. What were the men doing? They looked to be raising the portcullis. Was the shout perhaps a greeting? Had someone arrived?

"Someone has come," Guinevere said.

"I did not hear mention of anyone arriving," Elinor murmured. She was in charge of figuring out the plans for the castle and reporting back to Guinevere. She knew if a messenger had arrived, if a missive was sent, who came and went. She was quite adept at sneaking about and making friends with anyone who would talk.

"Perhaps they were not invited," Claudia said, a shiver in her voice.

Guinevere watched intently, listening for any unusual sounds. Her eyes continued to be drawn to the two guards raising the portcullis. They looked... different.

The men in the bailey below seemed to take notice of the portcullis being raised and they shouted to the men on duty. But the two opening the gate ignored them, no longer waving their hands in signal, but moving faster and faster with the portcullis ropes.

And that was when a shout of warning was issued by the guards in the bailey below. Men roused from barracks stumbled out just as a horde of savage warriors ran through the gate, swords drawn, their wild hair waving in the North Sea breeze. Legs exposed to the elements, slick with rain. They were violent in their entry, brutal in their attack on the tired English soldiers. Hacking and stabbing.

Guinevere's knees buckled and she grabbed hold of the windowsill for balance. They were under attack!

"Oh, heaven help us." Guinevere crossed herself. She had often wondered when such a thing would happen, not even *if* it would. Nay, there had never been a question of *if*.

Since their arrival at Dunnottar, the Scottish uprising had grown in strength. There were rumors of a warrior, a man who fought for the king, that he was as tall as an oak and as brave as iron. That he faced death daily and laughed in the devil's face. He'd been sacking one English-controlled castle in Scotland after another and most recently had gained a victory over the English at Stirling Bridge, nearly ten to one.

Was this he? Was this his horde?

"We are going to die," Claudia whispered.

"We must hide," Abigail said.

"We must run," Elinor countered. "There is an escape hatch. The drop is steep, but it leads to the stairs leading down to the beach. We will run and then we will hide."

"We'll never make it," Claudia said, hugging herself, her teeth chattering.

"We have no choice," Guinevere said. "We must try, or die without having at least attempted to save ourselves."

"Guin is right. Get your mantles on. We must go now before they breach the doors to the keep."

They hurried to tug on their mantles, and then headed for the door. The shouts of pain and death filled the bailey below and floated up through every window in the keep, surrounding them in a ghastly cloud.

"Where is the hatch?" Guinevere asked. "You lead the way."

She'd not done much exploring of the castle herself, preferring to keep to her chamber as much as possible. A mistake she now regretted.

"This way." Elinor grabbed a torch from the wall and hurried down the corridor toward the stairs.

They made it down one circular round to the floor below before the doors to the keep were breached. The stomping of boots, scrape of metal and cries of those in the main entryway struck their ears.

"Oh no." Claudia gripped the wall.

"Come, we can still make it," Elinor said. "'Tis just beyond the great hall."

They continued slowly down the stairs, trying not to make a sound. Breath held, hands fisted in their skirts, lifting the hems from their feet, Guinevere pushed her fears away, while Abigail whispered to Claudia to hush every time she whimpered.

They stepped off the stairs, faced by four doorways—one that led to the garrison below, one to the great hall, one toward the main doors and one to the kitchens.

But when Elinor reached for the iron handle leading to the great hall, the angry voice of Baron de Ros could be heard through the iron-studded door. "Who the bloody hell are you?" he shouted.

There was a low rumble of an answer and then the clashing sound of swords. Angry shouts. With every clang, Guinevere jumped.

Keep it together. Stay strong.

"We must hide." Guinevere pointed toward the great hall. "There is no way we're going in there and there is no other way to get to the hatch." She took a deep breath. "Back upstairs. We'll barricade ourselves in my chamber."

"Or mayhap we should dress as servants in the kitchen?" Claudia suggested. "Servants are less likely to be killed."

"But the Scottish servants already here will tell who we are." Abigail's lips were pinched thin, white in the torchlight.

"We must go back to my chamber," Guinevere said. "They are less likely to kill ladies, I should think."

"Did you see how uncivilized they were?" Claudia asked. "They'll hack us to bits without question."

Guinevere suppressed a shudder, her mind dredging up the images of the savages bursting through the gate and slicing into any man they saw. "All will be well." But her tone, no matter how calm she tried to make it, sounded decidedly shrill. And she was lying through her teeth.

Had she truly traversed all this way, made it thus far with hopes for widowhood or an annulment, to be murdered before her life had truly started?

"All will be well," Elinor murmured, nodding at Guinevere, a silent agreement to stay strong.

Claudia and Abigail mumbled the same, though the looks in their eyes was telling. The two of them were terrified, perhaps even more so than Guinevere.

"Pray, my ladies," Guinevere said. "God will protect us."

Hand in hand, they hurried up the stairs to Guinevere's chamber, barring the door.

"The wardrobe," Guinevere said.

She went to one side and Elinor to the other, but even the two of them pushing couldn't move the massive oak piece.

"Come help us." Guinevere's tone brooked no argument and Claudia and Abigail rushed to help.

With the effort of all four of them they were able to shove the mighty wardrobe in front of the door, completely covering it on both sides.

"That should hold them." Guinevere shuddered. She wasn't truly certain it would. The savage way they'd come through the gate only made her imagine that they'd hack their way through her door and then the wardrobe just to get at them. And surely the loud sounds of scraping must have drawn the attention of the warriors below.

"Pray don't let us die tonight," Guinevere said, gazing at the moonless sky as dark and forbidding as the savage warriors below.

CHAPTER THREE

Anything that seemed too easy, usually was.

At least that had always been Brody's belief. So why did it appear that besieging Dunnottar was *too easy*?

The sleepy English knights had been unprepared. Just as Wallace suspected, being in this remote location, the sun set and rain falling, they'd never suspected a thing.

Even when he and Wallace jumped down from the grassy knoll onto the gate house battlement, the men had seemed too surprised to even react. As though perhaps they had hoped it was all a bad dream. They stared up at Brody and Wallace like apparitions from the sky.

Brody almost didn't have the heart to smash in the man's skull until he recalled just want had happened to his da and sister, and then watching his blade sink into the man's eye socket had been a pleasure. An eye for an eye? Nay, he'd take the whole damn body.

After raising the gate, they'd had to fend off the other guards on the wall, most of whom seemed to be in their first month of training for none of them knew how to wield a sword properly. They'd climbed down to the bailey, fighting the lazy knights who clambered, half dressed, from their sleeping mats in the barracks.

There was not nearly four thousand men. Five hundred at most. Which meant either the bishop had been exaggerating or the general here had already sent his men out into the Highlands. No matter, if the bastard had sent his men out they would be welcomed back by the tip of his sword.

Brody stood in the great hall of Dunnottar now, his men fought a few lazy knights around the perimeter, Wallace still outside leading the fight against the English in the bailey.

"Surrender and we may yet let ye live," Brody said to the Sassenach noble who stood in the center of the great hall, eyes bloodshot enough to prove he'd had more than his fair share, and that of someone else, too, in ale or whisky.

"Never." The man raised his sword, wobbling on spindly legs.

He looked old enough to be a seasoned warrior, but the way he held his weapon, the lack of musculature on his person led Brody to believe he did more ordering about than actual fighting. His light hair was mussed and falling into his eyes and his clothes were disheveled, streaks of blood stained his shirt from cuts he'd sustained from fighting one of Brody's men. They'd woken the man, it seemed, from sleeping at the trestle table, and when his men had realized the man was one, too inebriated to fight fairly, and two, the general in charge, they'd summoned Brody inside.

"Might I have the pleasure of knowing your name?" Brody asked, keeping his voice calm and cordial, even though he expected to take this man's breath within the next few minutes, just as soon as he found out for certain he was the general in charge.

"Baron de Ros, General in His Majesty King Edward's army, and I demand you leave Dunnottar at once."

Brody cringed inwardly at the way his English accent butchered the name of the castle. "Ah, I suspected ye were of noble blood and a general, too. Do ye know General Gray?"

The man's eyes seemed to focus at Gray's name and he studied Brody with a bit more keen interest. "I do."

Brody grinned, feeling a rush through his blood. "Good enough."

"What?" The general wrinkled his brow, confusion clouding his feeble mind.

No matter, General Gray had showed no mercy to Johanna or Brody's father. And Brody would show no mercy now. "Any last words?"

"Last words…" Understanding dawned in the man's eyes and he turned in a slow circle to take in the dead English bodies around the room, and the looming, breathing bodies of the Scots, some who held a few English captive. "Aye."

"I will wait." Brody pressed the tip of his sword into the wood-planked floor.

"Goodbye." And with that, Baron de Ros turned around and fled toward the back of the great hall, the remaining English knights alive wrestled against the Scots.

Brody chuckled and nodded to his men. "Let them go after him. They will not get far."

They slipped through a back door leaving Brody and the men staring after them, perplexed mostly, but not entirely surprised.

"They have no honor," Brody muttered. 'Twas odd that they just run away from a battle. Well, he supposed they wouldn't be the first to retreat, but that didn't stop him for thinking less of the fools. "After them."

They raced toward the back of the great hall and through the small door leading past the buttery and kitchens. The door at the back of the kitchen slammed shut and several servants—all Scottish—pointed toward the door with trembling fingers.

Brody and his men pushed through into the kitchen gardens. The fools were trampling the herbs and vegetables as they scrambled toward the gate leading back toward the bailey. Surprisingly, none headed for the postern.

No matter, they could run, but they couldn't hide.

Except, they must have, for as soon as Brody made it through the gate, the men seemed to have disappeared.

Wallace stood in the center of the bailey, sweat and blood streaked over his shirt, staining dark in the firelight from a great bonfire.

"They've all taken refuge in the kirk," Wallace said.

"All?"

He chuckled. "I may have given them cause to do so."

"How?"

"Warned them that they'd best pray to God for forgiveness for I was their maker come to take them home to Hell."

Brody raised a brow and watched Wallace wipe his bloody claymore on his plaid.

"And they simply ran." Brody shook his head.

"More or less. Are ye surprised?"

"Nay, not at all." Given the men in the great hall had done the same, he expected nothing less. "What do ye plan to do with them?"

"As I said, I was going to send them back to Hell."

Brody followed Wallace's line of vision toward the newly erected kirk, not more than a few years old. The bishop had overseen its completion and consecration before being stormed by de Ros last year.

"We're going to storm the church?" Brody asked.

Wallace's gaze fell on the kirk, his brow furrowing, jaw set in a determined way. "We're going to burn it to the ground."

Brody might have had some misgivings about bringing death to a holy place by his sword—but actually burning the building? "Isn't that asking God for punishment?"

Wallace shook his head slowly, his face grim. "God wants us to see it done. His verra walls are poisoned by the sheer number of English bastards inside."

Flashes of Johanna's bruised, bloodied and prone body flashed in Brody's mind. The way her gown had been torn, her hair hacked away at her scalp, the way one lip hung slack, nearly torn from her face and the teeth marks surrounding the wound. A thirst, more potent than even that of a dying man, a hunger for revenge, battered around his veins. "I will help ye burn the bastards to the ground."

"I knew ye would." Wallace nodded to the bonfire. "Let us make torches."

"We'll need an agent to help with burning, so the rain doesn't cause the blazes to fizzle out." Brody snapped at two cowering servants by the wall. "Bring us oil and cooking lard." They hurried to do his bidding and gathered more able bodies along their way.

Seemed the Scottish servants were only too happy to oblige in the execution of their keepers, even if it meant burning a place of worship.

"Noah," Brody called. "Bar the kirk doors from the outside."

His cousin nodded, calling several men to follow him. They used a thick wooden bar from the main gates and threaded it through the church door handles. Moving to the windows, they nailed them shut.

Then the warriors grabbed logs, branches, anything that would burn, and carried them oiled and flamed toward the kirk. As Wallace shouted to the English to rot in Hell, they threw their torches to the roof and watched as the thatch quickly caught fire.

The English scrambled, the sounds of the shouts and banging on the door filling the night sky. But not one of the Scots moved to help. Instead, the two Scottish armies watched silently, grimly, as the flames grew and the sounds of those screaming inside grew deafening.

Brody hung his head, asking forgiveness for their sins, praying for the souls of his departed kin, praying that God would shun those they executed tonight.

But even when the shrieks from inside dissipated, Brody could still hear screams on the wind. Perhaps their souls rising up to the heavens? Or fighting the devil as he dragged them through the fires for all eternity?

Nay. These were true screams. Female cries.

He turned back toward the keep, listening. The horror-filled shrieks were coming from inside.

Did de Ros have a wife? A daughter?

God's teeth, but he'd not thought to check. So intent on chasing down de Ros, he'd not even bothered to make his rounds of the keep.

Unbidden, his pace quickened until he was running toward the keep with a mind to put an end to the incessant wail. He slammed through the front doors, searched out the stairs, rounding and stopping on each floor to listen, until he came to the third level. Certain the screams were coming from there, he marched down the dark, narrow corridor until the wails reached a fever pitch behind a door.

He tried the handle. Locked. Most likely barred, too.

He'd have to break it down.

Brody backed up to the far wall, took a deep breath, then kicked his heel out, slamming it against the handle. Wood splintered, the door shuddered, but did not open more than inch.

'Twas blocked.

Smart. If he were a lass at a castle undergoing a siege, he'd block it, too.

No matter. Brody was large, strong and would not let something like a piece of furniture get in his way.

He lifted his foot again, slamming his heel once more against the door, splintering it in the center and noting with satisfaction that it opened two more inches. He slammed his shoulder against the door now, feeling the weight of something large, perhaps a wardrobe, shift immensely. The screams grew louder, piercing his skull, but along with it hushed murmurings to contradict the incessant wails.

"Cease that noise!" he bellowed, shouldering the door once more.

The wardrobe teetered on its corners and fell forward with a loud boom, just as a thunderous boom outside echoed in the courtyard—the kirk had, no doubt, collapsed.

Brody pushed the door open the remainder of the way and came face to face with four Englishwomen. They huddled by the window, dressed in Sassenach gowns, hair once styled as though they were attending a great feast, jewels at their necks, and tears adorning each face except for one.

"Och, but I've died and gone to Hell," he muttered.

Everyone knew Englishwomen were as shrewish as... well as, an Englishwoman, and as cold as dead fish.

All four stared at him, wide-eyed, mouths hung agape.

Much like fish, he thought.

They were pretty enough, especially the one with the long flowing blonde locks. Though it looked as though her locks had seen better days, perhaps not to have been torn from whatever fancy knot they'd been in.

"Who are ye?" he asked in not too kind a tone. He didn't want any shrewish behavior, simply facts.

The blonde stepped forward, squared her shoulders and looked him straight in the eye with her piercing blue—nay more green than blue—eyes. She was the only one who didn't cry. As though she'd been expecting him. The lass was beautiful, even if she was a harpy. Her bone structure was delicate, but her eyes sharp, and the way she frowned, well, he guessed her tongue to be just as barbed. The gown accentuated the curve of her hips and the swell of marginal breasts—he refused to call them the perfect size, for she was English, and he denied finding anything about her to be flawless.

"Who are *you*?" she retorted.

Och, a fiery little fish. "I asked ye first."

"Well"—her gaze roved from the top of his head down to his boot tips and he felt more than a little assessed—"I think it is plain to see I outrank you, savage, so you must answer me first."

At her bold words the ladies in her presence all paled, one covered her mouth, another pinched her own arms and the third nodded approval.

Brody chuckled, taking a menacing step forward. "Then I suppose we have found ourselves at an impasse, fishy, for I do believe I outrank ye."

"Fishy? Ye insult me." She shook her head and regarded him with something akin to disgust. "Impossible."

Her revulsion almost had him checking himself. How odd, and why should he even wonder at her manners? She was English after all. Every woman he'd ever met up to this point had fallen at his feet. Brody was known for his charismatic tongue, his lovemaking abilities. Well, this fish wouldn't know those things. And from the looks of her, she'd be too uptight to enjoy the pleasures he could have given her, if he wanted to, which he wouldn't.

Brody puffed his chest and took several steps forward. "I assure ye, madam, given your current situation, *anything* is possible."

Two of her ladies fainted dead away and the third stepped in front of the blonde, only to be shoved behind, a sharp word from the Grande Fishy's mouth.

Then she turned back to him, pursing her lips as though she were contemplating a truce.

Before she could speak, he cut her off. "I dinna make deals, lass. If ye dinna believe me, then take a look out your window at the kirk yonder."

"So you intend to kill us then?" Despite the stubborn set to her jaw and shoulders, her lower lip quivered.

Och, but why did that slight tremble have to tug at his heart? "We shall see what comes to pass."

Her eyes widened slightly. "You would kill innocent women?"

"Your ilk has done no less but the same," Brody growled. An eye for an eye, is that not what he'd been taught? Is that not what war was all about?

Her life for his sister's.

She chewed her lip nervously, waiting for him to answer, to decide her fate.

Perhaps there is a wench for ye to take to wife... Wallace's words returned to him, sharp and insistent. *Blasphemous!* Brody thrust them aside, fisting his hands at his side.

"I will do as I see fit." His voice came out harsh, cruel. And he should do as he saw fit. But could he take his revenge for his sister out on a woman that was, for all intents and purposes, innocent of that crime?

The thought of slitting her pretty, white throat left a rather bitter taste on his tongue. He could not stoop to the level of the English bastards.

Brody examined her. He'd never been this close to an Englishwoman before. His accounts of what they were like only came secondhand—even from that of Wallace. She was truly stunning, if not pallid from fear. Her eyes were a mesmerizing mixture of blue and green, and her hair looked golden in the light of the fire. She was of a good height, perhaps coming to his shoulder. She had high cheekbones, a defined, but not square jaw, and lips the color of pink roses in summer. Her tiny red tongue kept darting out to lick those lips, making his blood run a little hotter than it should for a woman of her breeding.

If she'd been Scottish, perhaps he would have considered taking her as his wife, for begrudgingly, he did desire her, would have had fun undressing her, taking her to bed.

"Come closer," he demanded.

She shook her head. "I'll not be your prize, a reward for the murder you have committed this night." Her voice came out stronger than before.

Brody sucked his teeth. "Come closer or I shall be forced to drag ye closer myself."

The lady behind her whispered something, but the lass shook her head. She smoothed her hands on the front of her gown and took a tentative step closer. Her skin had taken on a rather gray pallor and he feared she might also faint. Her hands trembled, and judging from the way her skirts vibrated, her knees must have been knocking together, too.

But still, she came closer, perhaps defying herself, most certainly defying his own assumptions.

When she was within inches of him, he reached out and skimmed his fingers along her cheek.

"It is as they say," he murmured. "Ye English wenches are as cold as ice. But ye dinna smell like a fish."

43

Her mouth parted in shock, arms crossing protectively and she retorted, quite haughtily, "Well, you don't smell like death, though that's what you bring."

CHAPTER FOUR

Her mouth was dry.

Dryer than if she'd put sand on her tongue. Or like any time she disappointed her father.

Her knees knocked together so fiercely she swore the Highlander before her could hear the sound echoing, as though her legs had decided they were mighty oaks and her knees woodpeckers drumming for their supper.

What was she thinking speaking to him that way?

Guinevere stared up at him, blinking, trying to bring him into view. Her head swirled and it was all she could do to concentrate on standing rather than collapsing. She'd never stood up for herself with her husband, nor her father. Nay, Guinevere did what she was told.

45

What had come over her? Why now, with this man, trained for killing? This barbarian?

Everything about him screamed ferocious, and yet... His fingers on her face were warm, even if they were rough.

Guinevere tightened her hold on her skirts, afraid she might rip them, but that tightness also kept her standing. She'd not missed the blood-tinged tip of the sword at his hip or the hilt of the small dagger in his sock. He was no doubt covered in weapons from head to toe. Ready to slay anyone who batted a lash. For that reason, she kept her eyes wide, which, of course, only made them water, for need to blink. From what she'd heard of the men's tales of battle, the heathen Scots wore weapons as a second skin. Beneath his shirt and wool plaid he was likely wearing a suit of daggers. Anything that might cut and maim.

Had she willingly walking to her death?

What were all his comments about fish?

She was so confused.

Partly so at him, but mostly at her own bold rashness. This was madness. She should turn and run. Perhaps encourage her ladies to leap from the window, for certainly he brought with him a worse fate.

The warrior said nothing, simply stared at her with an intensity she found unnerving as he stroked her face. The time allowed her eyes to calm their watering, her knees to stop knocking, her hands to stop trembling, and finally, she was able to concentrate on something more than standing up.

She stared into his eyes, gray, rimmed with blue, thick lashes, and eyebrows that slashed across his forehead like two dark sword blades.

His hair, black as night, was pulled back in a queue. Sweat trickled along the edges of his temples, beaded his tanned brow.

He did not smile. And, in fact, his lips were so harsh looking, she wasn't certain he was one to ever turn his lip up. Perhaps a perpetual frowner.

Despite the wildness of his slashing features, he was handsome. Incredibly so. Guinevere drew in a deep, deep breath. Prepared to say something about him calling her a fish. Or alluding to her having anything to do with a slimy, stinky creature of the sea, but her throat was still slightly swollen, and her voice refused to work.

"Mayhap when they say Englishwomen are as cold as fishes they mean those in the deep dark sea. A nymph," he murmured, tracing the line of her jaw—a feeling she didn't find altogether unpleasant which sent a fresh wave of fear washing over her. "A fairy fish."

The Highlander shook himself and jerked his hand away from her face as though she'd burned him. Or perhaps he was afraid she'd turn him into a fish. He seemed obsessed with the notion that she was not a creature of the water. Mayhap the man was addled.

In which case, he was even more threatening than she'd previously assumed. A man not in full capacity of his contemplations and speculations was extremely dangerous.

She took a step back, wishing she'd done as her mother suggested when she'd left England and worn a dagger up her sleeve at all times. But whenever she'd done that, the pointed end always poked her skin. More so, perhaps, she should have taken her mother's advice to never approach a Scottish warrior. She'd never really been that good at listening to her mother's advice.

And, well, unfortunately, it was a little late to decide she'd have taken a permanent blister from poked skin in order to whip the weapon out now.

Blast it all!

Finally finding her voice, she planted her hands on her hip and said, "Are you going to stare at me all day or exact my punishment?"

"And what crime have ye committed?" He looked at her expectantly, as though he eagerly waited for her to confess her sins.

"You are no confessor," she said, setting her jaw. "I see no point in giving you a detailed report. 'Tis obvious, you've come to besiege the castle. We are enemies. Is it not only natural for you to punish us all?" Dear heavens, where was this boldness coming from?

The warrior leveled his gray-blue gaze on her and crossed thick arms over a massive chest. "And what if I was the last man to hear your thoughts?"

Guinevere tore her regard away from his strong arms and flashed her gaze over his forehead. Trying for any medium place to rest her gaze than his dangerously beautiful eyes or mesmerizing strength. "Then I'd be doomed to hell, for I'm certain you are a heathen." This time when she spoke her voice came out harsh.

Brody chuckled, the sound low and scarping along her nerves in a way that wasn't... terrible. "Ye call me a heathen when your countrymen are ransacking my country? Killing my men. Raping my women. Desecrating holy ground."

Oh, but that made her mad! Was he not doing the very same thing. She slammed her hand against his chest before realizing what she was doing, and grabbed her own arm back, clutching it to her chest. Still, he didn't immediately kill her, so she decided to jab him with her words. "You savages are the ones burning the church. Killing the knights—" Guinevere's mouth fell open as she realized the last of his accusations—rape, he'd not yet committed.

Yet.

Was that next? Was that why he'd tested her temperature?

"Have ye more to say?" He urged, with eyebrows jutted toward his hairline. "I'm ever so interested to hear the rest of it, lass."

Guinevere swallowed the bile that had risen in her throat. The scent of the great fire, the thick smoke, it swirled in the air. She wanted to close her eyes, drop to her knees in prayer, and yet behind her, one of her ladies whimpered. "I've nothing further to say," she managed to keep her tone strong, even haughty. "Only that you must leave. Now."

The Scot grinned, a hungry looking expression. "Ah, so we are back to who outranks who and who must listen to whom."

For an addled man, he certainly had a way with words and she tried not to be captivated by the lovely sound of his burr. The smooth and roughness of it. Saints, but it was stroking over her in a way that was almost hypnotizing. *Stop it! He is the enemy!* And yet, he'd only challenged her with his words, nothing to harm her physically.

Yet. *Stop being a ninny!*

Again she straightened to her full height, which was no match for his. Her hands returned to her hips and she met his gaze head on. "If you must hurt someone, hurt me and leave my women be."

"Hurt." The word rolled over his tongue in a contemplative tone. Then he frowned. But not just any frown. A grimace. A painful contortion that made her heart constrict. "Ye insult me," he ground out. "If I wasn't worried your maids would die of shock, I'd pull ye over my knee and spank your bare arse, and still ye'd not know the worst of what your countrymen have done."

Guinevere gasped, her hand coming to her throat and she backed up a step. Her breath stayed in her lungs, unable to escape, her throat constricted and her heart lurched. No one had dared to thrash her since she was a child, and only because she'd stolen a pie Cook had made for her father's birthday and she'd eaten the entire thing, then lied about it—with the evidence still all over her face.

The Highlander bared his teeth at her and she was afraid, instead of thrashing her, he might just bite her. Swallow her whole. But he didn't. He chomped his teeth at her, making a clicking sound and then whirled on his heel, storming from the chamber, the floor shaking beneath his powerful stomps. He slammed the broken door, which only bounced back open, where it hung loosely at the hinge, to show the empty corridor beyond. Every bone in her body was rattled, her nerves frayed, her senses left unhinged.

Guinevere sank to the floor, still clinging to her neck, gasping for air, her stays suddenly so very tight, her throat swollen, the air hot and unbearable.

She tugged at her dress, wanting desperately to be rid of anything touching her skin.

Elinor rushed to her side with a cup of wine, Claudia and Abigail still unconscious on the floor.

"My lady," she murmured, dropping to Guinevere's side. She tucked Guinevere against her own shoulder. Elinor held the cup to her lips and Guinevere drank greedily, desperate to take the edge off. "Guin, are you all right?"

She shook her head, her entire body shaking. It had taken so much strength to stand up to him. "We've not seen the last of him. He will be back."

"Aye." Elinor's voice was quiet, resolute.

"We have to try to escape again while the barbarians are by the kirk, watching it burn. We need to get to the hatch and run."

They helped each other to stand and threw water from the basin onto Claudia and Abigail's faces. There was no time for a gentle wakening. Her friends needed to be alert and quick.

They roused, touching their heads that no doubt hurt, and rubbing at their eyes that were no doubt blurred. Elinor gave them a linen to wipe the water from their faces.

"We must go. He will be back," Guinevere urged.

She and Elinor helped the two to their feet and just as they had before, the four of them rushed from the room. This time, Elinor urged them to take the servants stairs on the second level leading down to the kitchens. From there, they peeked into the great hall, the floor strewn with bodies.

Guinevere looked, not seeing her husband at all. Had he escaped? Was he still alive?

And then, because she'd been wondering it all along, she glanced toward the entryway, wondering with dread, had he burned in the church?

She shuddered. Aye, she did not want to be married to him, but neither did she want him to suffer tremendously. He'd done some horrible things, aye, and now the Scots had come seeking revenge.

Perhaps the Lord had been kind and taken away their pain as they burned. But judging from the sounds of the screams, she knew that not to be the case.

Guinevere shook the gory thoughts from her mind and thanked her lucky stars that the Highland warrior had not seen fit to lop her head off with his bloody sword. But he had given her another chance to escape.

Elinor tugged her down a dank corridor, the scents of blood and fear melting off the stone. Or maybe that was just her and her ladies. Every part of her vibrated with fear. An energy pummeling her limbs and making her tremble.

They found the hatch, a grate in the stone, large enough for a man to drop through, that opened to the thick grasses twenty feet below. Elinor tugged at the opening, but an iron lock was sturdily in place. Guinevere dropped to her knees and yanked at the lock, not that it did any good.

"There's no use," Claudia murmured.

"We are going to die," Abigail said.

"Will you ninnies quit it?" Elinor scolded. "Nothing but naysayers, the both of you."

Guinevere didn't speak. Part of her mind hummed the same warnings, another part shouted Elinor's response in order to get her mind to shut up.

"A key. We need a key," Guinevere said.

But she wasn't certain the baron had ever had a key. She'd heard no mention of it. Nor had she ever seen anyone use the hatch. "Elinor, did you happen to hear of a key?"

Elinor nodded slowly. "I believe there was a rack in the library, the room where all the scrolls and books the monks had been working on was. On the rack were dozens of keys."

"I will go get them," Guinevere said.

"Nay, you cannot go alone," Elinor said.

Guinevere glanced at Claudia and Abigail. "You both stay here. Hidden. We'll be back shortly."

"But we've only one torch," Abigail said, her teeth chattering.

"Aye. And no one will see you sitting here in the dark. You'll be safer that way. Safely hidden."

The truth was, Guinevere was afraid that if they came along, the two would only give way to wails that would be a beacon for any other savages pushing through the doors. Who knew if any other barbarian would have the same restraint that the large, dark, handsome one had.

Handsome.

How could she even think something like that?

Well, he was. Perhaps in a rugged sort of way, but she could not think such thoughts. He was her enemy—even if he'd done her no harm.

Elinor tugged Guinevere away before Claudia and Abigail could protest. They slinked up the servants stairs to the next level and found the library open and quiet.

The men had yet to ransack the place, but time was ticking and it wouldn't be long before the intrigue of the fire dissipated and they went in search of more jovial pursuits. Say, perhaps four English women with no protector.

The hook with a dozen keys was just were Elinor had said it would be.

"We'll take them all." Guinevere plucked each one down, filling her hand with them.

Her eyes caught on a wax seal breaker on the desk amid the missives and scrolls. It was sharp like a dagger and the only weapon at her disposal. She grabbed that, too. Though it had been many years since her father had showed her how to thrust a blade, she was pretty certain in a pinch she could see the deed done.

They hurried back down the stairs toward the kitchen, stopping when they heard the deep baritone of male voices coming from the great hall.

"They come." Guinevere shuddered.

But the women didn't let that stop them. They hurried to the other side of the kitchen and the back walkway servants used to get from room to room until they returned to the hatch, their torch lighting on Claudia and Abigail still clutching on to each other, silent screams on their lips.

With no time to waste before the men began searching the castle, especially if the warrior had told everyone about her and her ladies, Guinevere ducked down and began inserting one key after another into the lock. It wasn't until she came to the ninth key that she found a match. It slid easily inside and twisted, a resounding click allowing her to breathe a sigh of relief.

They were so close to escaping this nightmare. The stench of burning. The savages ready to pounce.

"Pray, my ladies." Guinevere glanced up at each of them. "No matter what happens, know that I was grateful for all you did for me."

"Don't speak like that," Elinor said, her hand trembling and making the torchlight bounce.

Guinevere brace herself against the weight of the grate and opened the hatch, the hinge creaking, the sound echoing through the small space and certain to bring those in the great hall running.

But she wasn't going to wait around to see when they'd show up.

Sunlight filtered up from the hatch. At some point when she'd been searching for the keys, dawn had broken.

She nodded to her women and let her legs dangle in the hole. The drop was far. Perhaps fifteen feet. She'd never fallen so far before in her life and she feared breaking a leg or twisting her ankle, but what other choice did she have?

Sucking in a breath, she scooted her rear forward and let herself drop into oblivion. She tucked up her legs, remembering some fact from when she was a child climbing trees that if you bent your knees you stood less a chance of breaking a leg.

The landing was harsh and she let out an oomph, quickly rolling out of the way of Claudia who followed, her hands over her mouth to cover her scream. Abigail was next, her dress stuffed into her mouth, and still a mournful wail escaped. Last was Elinor, who dropped with perfect ease, landing with a roll. She'd grown up with many brothers and Guinevere wouldn't have been surprised if this wasn't the first hatch she'd leapt through.

By sheer luck, or the grace of God, they had no major injuries between them other than sore bottoms and a slight twinge in Abigail's ankle, though she said it didn't pain her as much as a sprain would.

Outside of the castle, there were two choices: the steep stairs to the beach that sat fifty feet or so to their left, or jumping off the cliff to certain death. To the beach it was. If only she'd taken more interest in sailing, maybe, just maybe, they could have taken one of the de Ros ships and set them on a course back to England. Alas, she didn't know the first thing about how a ship worked.

The grass was slippery and they each tripped more than once as they scrambled to the stairs, just waiting for men to drop from the hatch to capture them.

Just as their feet hit the stairs, a shout echoed from the hatch. Oh, dear, heavens, they would be found. They flew down the slippery rocks at a rate that was only a whisper away from a death wish.

A thud from above. Someone had dropped through the hatch.

"Down," she whispered. "They will not see us if we crouch."

Crouched low, they continued their descent of the steep rock staircase, grateful that it had been carved deep from the mountain itself affording a wall of sorts on both sides. But crouching made them go slower and by the time they made it to the beach, the sound of boots on stone above were closer and closer.

"There is a cave," Elinor said, through gasping breaths.

Guinevere didn't ask how Elinor knew about it, though she could guess. Her lady was adept at gathering secrets, but also men.

"Stick to the sides of the mountain where the weeds grow so they cannot see our footprints," Guinevere said. And she prayed it was enough to keep the heathens at bay.

CHAPTER FIVE

Brody walked patiently across the beach. Or rather, with as much patience as he could garner.

When he'd left the wenches in their chamber he'd not thought they had enough gumption to traverse the castle looking for a means of escape. He supposed he could admit to underestimating them, though it irked him to do so.

They'd been quiet in their escape, he'd give them that. He'd not have suspected before that English wenches would have the ability to be so silent. Especially not when the leader of their foursome had been so mouthy.

He followed the path of their footprints along the base of the cliff. That was smart, for he probably wouldn't have

57

looked there if he'd not seen flashes of feminine heads and gowns scurrying down the roughly cut stone stairs.

The scent of burning wood and bodies still soaked the sea-misted air. Brody's nostrils felt singed from it. 'Twas distasteful in his own opinion, but he'd not disparage the leader of the rebellion. The English were vile, vicious wastrels. Murderers. Wallace had a lot of anger, but so did Brody. He wanted blood, revenge, the damned English off Scottish soil, too, but he wanted to fight them. He wanted to draw blood with his sword, not burn them all in a building when their backs were turned. That was a coward's way out. That was the English way.

He tried to shake the thoughts from his mind, but they remained somewhere in the background.

Then he had an unsettling thought. What would Wallace and the rest of the bloodthirsty warriors do with the four English women when Brody brought them back to the castle?

Their fate would not be pleasant, he knew that for a fact.

Because that notion had been niggling in his brain since he'd first found them, he'd gone through the hatch secretly and with only Noah by his side—the solitary person he trusted fully.

Brody nodded to his cousin, pointing toward the mouth of a cave where the footprints ended.

They drew their swords, just in case the English fishes had found some hidden *Sassenach* to protect them.

The cave was dark, but not deep enough to hide the four women huddled together. The lady, whom he'd had the unfortunate, unpleasant encounter with before, stood in front, a small dagger held out in her steady hand.

Steady.

She was a fighter.

Another glowing attribute he did not want to acknowledge.

"Leave us be," she ordered.

Brody sheathed his sword, nodding to his cousin to do the same, and then he held out his hands to the sides—just as he would when approaching a rabid dog or injured horse.

"My lady, I promised I'd not hurt ye before and I dinna intend to go back on my word. I am Brody Keith, Marischal of Scotland, Laird and Chief of Clan Keith. This is my cousin and second, Noah Keith."

The lady eyed them warily, inching back, though she had nowhere to go. The dagger shook for a split second before she steadied her nerves.

Amazing.

"I will not say that it is nice to meet you." She jutted her chin.

"And I dinna require it."

"What do you require? Not that I'm of a mind to abide."

Brody frowned. What was he going to do with these ladies? The thought had yet to cross his mind, only that he couldn't allow them to escape. That four, essentially unarmed, English women wouldn't last a day in the wilds of Scotland. Especially not with the Scottish warriors still bent on blood and needing a way to slake their lust.

It wasn't like he and Noah could toss them onto their two horses and take them back to their castle in East Lothian. Brody wasn't even certain when he was going back. Dunnottar was his and he was meant to fortify it before heading back to the border with Wallace.

These fishes had no champions now. Not with all the *Sassenach* warriors dead.

No champions but him and Noah.

Bloody hell...

Brody blew out a long, irritated breath. "I require ye to listen. To trust me."

The lady laughed, a bitter sound that scraped from her throat, filled with more derision than what she must have felt simply for him.

"You're a fool," she said.

"Perhaps I am. For there are six thousand Scots up on that cliff and but two of us."

"Two of you? You are Scots. Are you not with them?"

"Aye, I am with them. William Wallace is the Guardian of Scotland, we serve the same master. We want the same things for our country. But I did not burn the church." Why was he telling her this? He should shut his mouth now. "The men, their blood is raging, their need to slake a thirst could be taken out on ye."

The lass met his gaze square on. "You mean, they'd want to rape me and my ladies."

Brody nodded solemnly. "I won't rape ye. I'm offering ye my protection. Dunnottar is now mine, as is anything within it. I'll not allow them to harm ye."

Her shoulders squared and the small dagger came up a notch or two. "What are you insinuating?"

"I insinuate nothing. I am stating a fact."

She shook her head, waving the knife. "I need you to clarify."

"Clarify what?" Was she daft? He studied her, the angles of her features, the slope of her neck, the defiant set of her shoulders.

"You say that all within it is yours. Are you…" She swallowed, looking toward the cave walls before flicking her gaze back at him. "Are you trying to stake a claim to me? I am already married."

"Your husband was the constable here, aye?" Brody asked.

Her lower lip trembled. "Aye."

"Then I must inform ye, he is dead. Ye are no longer married."

His news did not shock her. She merely nodded. Behind her, two of her women trembled uncontrollably and he was afraid one or both of them would faint. The third glared at him and Noah with such ferocity he wondered if she could be related in any way to Lady de Ros.

"What is your name?" he asked her.

She straightened enough that he was now certain her spine would snap. "Lady Guinevere de Ros."

Brody didn't know why, but to hear her say de Ros' name in connection with hers… He didn't like it at all.

"No longer. Ye're now mine." The words were acid on his tongue. He'd not wanted a wife. Ever. Not wanted any more responsibility than he already had. The guilt of his sister and father's deaths was too heavy. He should have been able to save them. And he couldn't. He'd devoted the rest of his life to one cause and he didn't need another. His blood was too hot for revenge. To find the man who'd killed his father, raped and murdered his sister. He didn't have time for a wife—an English one at that.

Again the scrape of a bitter laughter came from her. "You think you can just stake your claim on me? I don't think so. I refuse."

Brody let out a low, frustrated growl. "Ye have no choice."

"I would rather die. Send me out to the sea to try to make it with the other fish."

"Ye will not die, my lady, for I will not kill ye, nor send ye out to sea. The men above, they will not kill ye either, at least not right away."

"I will kill myself, then." She held the dagger to her throat, the burn of vengeance in her eyes so deep he believed she would do it. Behind her, all three ladies shouted, "*Nay!*"

Brody took a small step forward, arms still outstretched and stopped within a distance in which he could easily reach for her.

"Then I must appeal to the protective side of ye, for I can see ye have one. The lady just there"—he pointed to the obstinate one—"she might follow in your footsteps, but the other two"—he shook his head —"they will not. And so if ye take yourself from this life, a grievous sin, then ye will also condemn them to a fate no one should suffer." Flashes of Johanna's torn body assaulted him and he had to close his eyes a moment to push them away.

But it was long enough for her to pick up on his grief.

"Someone has wronged you," she whispered, taking note of his second of grief, not something he'd wanted to reveal.

"Ye know nothing of me, other than I offer ye protection, an offer that does have an expiration. I've not slept in days and now that we've rid the castle of vermin, I'm eager to find a bed."

"If I accept your offer..." Her voice cracked and she swallowed hard. "If I consent to be your wife, what will become of my ladies?"

Brody shrugged, uncertain of what she was reaching for. "They will continue to serve ye."

She shook her head, removed the knife from her neck. "Can they be sent back to England?"

"Nay!" the strong one countered, but the other two nodded.

"If that is what ye wish."

"I do." She turned and whispered something to her lady, placing her hand on her shoulder. Whatever words she spoke seemed to calm her and he itched to know what they were. She turned her attention back to him. "I have another request."

The fact that she used the word request rather than demand was intriguing. Perhaps he was not the only one used to dealing with volatile creatures.

"Aye?"

"I would like to—" She cut herself off, chewed her lip and refused to meet his gaze. "Speak to you in private a moment."

What the devil? Brody nodded and motioned for Noah to go and stand with the ladies while he took hold of Guinevere's elbow. He guided her toward the mouth of the cave, though he didn't dare go out in case they were spotted before a deal was struck.

He crossed his arms over his chest and waited for her to make her desires known.

She drew in a deep breath and let it out slowly. Whatever her request, she was nervous to state it.

"Tell me." He glanced behind him, hoping she'd guess at his urgency. "As I said, the clock is ticking."

"I would agree to a… binding with you, but… I would wait to…" She waved her hand and it seemed as though she wanted him to guess the remainder.

Well, he had no bloody clue. Women were a mystery to him. He raised a questioning brow. "Wait to send your ladies?"

"Nay." She looked disappointed he'd guessed incorrectly.

"I must inform ye, lass, I'm not a mind reader. I grew up with sisters but not once was I able to discern their thoughts."

The poor lass' face flamed red and she rolled her eyes upward, staring at the roof of the cave. "I do not want to… share your bed. Or whatever form of sleeping habits you might have."

"We will sleep separately." That worked better for him, too, as he was certain she'd try to kill him as soon as he closed his eyes.

She pressed her lips together and he could tell she was frustrated. "What is it?" he asked, growing irritated. This was taking far too long. Did she not understand he had offered her and her ladies his protection, which he didn't need to do and would pose far greater a burden to him than it did her?

"I would wait several months before we consummate," she finally blurted out.

"Ah," Brody said, frowning. He'd not even contemplated that part himself. "Ye wish to see if ye carry the bastard's child?"

She frowned in answer.

"I suppose that is customary and a good idea as I dinna want to raise an English bastard's child."

"I am English."

He waved away her words. "Ye'll be Scottish if ye marry me."

"I don't think that is how it works."

"It bloody well is now," he retorted.

She raised her eyebrows, the tip of her pink tongue darting out to touch her top lip as though she were about to burn his ears with her words, but she quickly clamped her mouth shut, silent.

Hmm…

"And if I am?" she asked. There was a hard look in her eyes, as though she were baiting him into a trap.

"Then we'll deal with that when it comes to pass. Send the bairn to England or a convent."

The ire that filled her face told him that wasn't exactly the answer she'd been searching for, but she didn't say otherwise.

"Are we in agreement, then?" he asked. "The sun has well risen and the men will begin celebrating their success. I would have the four of ye inside, safe, than out here."

She pursed her lips. "We are in agreement."

"A blood bond is required."

Her face paled of the red hue her cheeks had taken on. "Blood bond?"

"If ye would not allow me entry to your bed for three months, then I require a blood bond." He grabbed the dagger from her hand and she jerked back a step. "Dinna be afraid." He pricked the tip of his finger. "Now ye."

Hesitantly, she held out her hand to him and he pricked her finger, a drop of blood quickly surfacing with her cry of pain.

"Man and wife," Brody said, pressing his bloody finger to hers. "With these four witnesses, I declare myself to ye. I will protect ye, honor ye, be your wedded husband."

Guinevere's trembling finger was still against his, her eyes wide as she stared up at him. She'd grown so pale, he feared she may faint. A few feet away, two of her ladies sobbed. Though quiet, it still echoed. Noah stared on with a matching horrified face as her obstinate lady.

"Now ye say the words," he drawled. "This is our wedding after all."

"Our wedding…" She swayed.

He reached forward, his hand on her waist to steady her, feeling the swell of her hips beneath his fingers.

"Aye. We'll see it properly done soon enough, but for now, under Highland law, this will suffice."

"All right."

He slid his hand to her hip and gave a small squeeze of encouragement.

"I declare myself your wife. I will protect ye, honor ye and be your wedded wife."

Brody grunted, those were the man's words, not the woman's. "And what about obedience?"

"What about it?" she countered.

He had to keep himself from laughing. This *iasg beag* (little fish) was going to give him a run for his sanity, he was certain. And he was kind of looking forward to it. The other part of him was screaming in horror and plotting different ways in which he could convince Wallace they should leave sooner to go to the front.

"All right, *iasg beag*, we are wed."

She opened her mouth to say something, but Brody didn't let her. Instead, he hauled her up against him, taking a moment to appreciate the lushness of her warm body, and then crushed his mouth to hers in a possessive kiss—silencing her words and tormenting himself with the knowledge he'd agreed to wait three months before taking her to bed.

CHAPTER SIX

Guinevere didn't know whether to be shocked, intrigued, offended. Perhaps all three.

Brody's lips were warm and firm, off-setting the coldness that had suffused her skin since the moment she'd first seen the fire raging in the kirk. The bellows of war, the savages crushing the English as though they were made of parchment.

She didn't lean into the warrior, not wanting him to think she was enjoying the soft slide of his mouth on hers. The possessive way in which he held her. The demanding curiosity that knocked inside her. But it didn't matter, the way his palm was firmly anchored on her waist, there was little moving away. And then his tongue swiped over hers.

She'd expected him to taste bitter—as acrid as the atmosphere surrounding them—and she was surprised he did not. Instead, the powerful laird who'd just declared her his wife tasted the exact opposite. Honey, sweetness, and spice. Of pleasant things, leaving her feeling wistful and euphoric. A kiss that left her mind floating away from this cave, the death and destruction, and going to a place she'd never been before.

She had guessed that kissing him would be as it had been with her husband—a rough, awkward clanking of teeth and licking of an unsettling, overly wet tongue, like that of a rambunctious dog. A rabid dog maybe. That she would be pawed and mauled and left curled in a suffering ball. Again, she was wrong. He did not clatter his teeth on hers. His tongue was the perfect combination of velvet and vapor. And the way he stroked her with it... Her body came alive, all heat and languid pleasure. Her nipples hardened and goose flesh rose with every flutter of her belly, every shiver of her limbs.

Except, that shouldn't be how she felt.

Not in this situation.

Nay, she should be shoving him away. Poking him with the tiny wax seal breaker. Telling him to get the hell away from her, that she'd agreed to this farce only to save her friends, herself, not so he could kiss her—however delicious it was.

He'd almost gotten away with whatever mind magic he was attempting to play with her. Almost. But, miraculously, or unfortunately, for perhaps it would have been nice to continue floating away from the present, she still had some wits about her.

Guinevere pressed her hands to his firmly muscled chest, breathing in one last time the hardy, powerful, masculine scent of him and then, she gave a little shove. Needing distance. Needing space to catch her breath. Needing a moment to rethink what had happened. Was there a way to undo this? Certainly a man that kissed like that was dangerous... A man like that was experienced. Would seek to seduce her. Would know she was not all she seemed.

He was not a man she'd want to give her virginity to. Not the man she'd been saving herself for—just as her husband had not been.

She backed away, wiping her mouth on her sleeve as though what had just transpired was so very unpleasant. Because she was a lady, she did refrain from spitting.

Brody raised his brows, the corner of his lip upturned. She didn't want to think about that expression, the way he must be mocking her for kissing him back. For knowing that she'd enjoyed it and lied about it now.

Her ladies and his cousin were silent, as though waiting for how they should react. Or perhaps they were too stunned to speak.

Guinevere grimaced, knowing she must at least act the part of an obedient wife, even if she'd already made it clear that she'd give him trouble if he asked for it.

So, pretending she'd not just swiped at her mouth like a toddler deciding they didn't like their stew, she curtsied to Brody.

"I am in your debt, my laird."

The ignorant beast simply grunted in response and she bristled. Most likely, he wasn't buying her charade. And there was no retort she could shout, for she had lied and she was in his debt. Furthermore, she was grateful that he'd been willing to marry her. That he'd been willing to go against his men's wishes, with the possibility of making many angry, and offer her and her ladies protection. She was even more grateful he'd agreed to wait three months before bedding her—even if he was lying. In those three months, but hopefully less, she planned on figuring a way out of this. She'd not let him steal her virtue as his horde of heathens had stolen her home.

"My lady," Noah said, stepping forward. He pulled out his sword and she took a step back. But she needn't have been so worried. He pressed the hilt to his chest and knelt on the sandy cave floor. "May I be the first to congratulate ye on your marriage to the Marischal Keith and to offer my loyalty as your subject."

Guinevere nodded, uncertain how to respond. None of the de Ros men had ever knelt before her. They respected her well enough as the wife of their overlord, but that was about it. Mostly, they just ignored her. It was hard for a woman to find her place in a man's world. Dunnottar was no ordinary castle. The lands were dangerous and the people more so. She'd had a hard time adjusting and most of the order of the castle had been directed by de Ros as he thought he knew better. Which, she'd not argued against because it gave her more time to do the things she did feel comfortable with and necessary.

How very different were the customs between their two worlds? Would Brody expect her to run the castle? Expect her to know the ins and outs of it all?

"Thank you," she murmured.

"Let's go," Brody said gruffly. "We will soon be missed and I'd rather get this over with sooner than later."

71

Get this over with... He meant telling his overlord that he'd married without permission. Saints, but she didn't want to be present for that. Hoped he'd let her lock herself away before then.

Brody took hold of her elbow and she tried to subtly pry herself free, but he held tight, narrowing his eyes in a no-nonsense sort of way. She refrained from sticking her tongue out.

"Come, ladies," Noah called as though her women were dogs. He ushered them to stand behind her and Brody, and then took up the rear.

With no further words, Brody half-dragged her down the beach as every few moments a wave of panic forced her to try and flee. And even when she did walk beside him she could barely keep up. His steps were easily twice as long as hers, and with only one hand to hold up the hem of her gown, she continued to slip in the sand.

Once they made it to the stairs, so narrow they could no longer walk side by side, he did push her behind him, though he held on to her hand with his. The flight up was much harder than it was on the way down. Her thighs and calves burned and her lungs felt ready to burst by the time she reached the top. With annoyance, she took note that her new husband did not even seem to break a sweat from climbing one hundred sixty steps.

Guinevere paused to catch her breath, forcing him to cease his movement. He stared at her as though she were ill, but waited nonetheless. His easy acceptance of her need to rest only irritated her more. Why should he be so accommodating?

She frowned. And why couldn't she climb some steps without nearly dying at the end? That thought almost made her laugh as she looked down over the cliff, taking in the steep drop. He was lucky she'd not made him rest halfway up. Or carry her.

Still, she wanted to be able to one day make that climb without nearly dying of exhaustion at the end.

Perhaps to bide her time she'd practice climbing these steps until she no longer seemed affected by it, even if it took her the rest of her days.

To the postern they went, a man on top calling down.

"Marischal! What have ye got there? A few tarts for the men?"

Guinevere bit her tongue and her ladies gasped behind her. Brody had been right, not that she'd doubted him. The men would want to celebrate using their bodies. As much as she regretted becoming the wife of a barbarian, at least she had spared herself and her ladies that horrid fate. Well, for three months at least.

"Nay. Open the gate." Brody's tone was not as jovial as the warrior's had been.

"I was only jesting," the guard grumbled.

The postern gate opened with a grating scrape of metal and wood, allowing them entry.

Brody hauled her up beside him, his heavy arm slinging over her shoulder, weighing her down slightly. They entered through the gate and into the rear bailey.

Several men stood from where they sat around cleaning their weapons and drinking straight from wine jugs that must have come out of her cellar. The spoils of war.

Except, weren't they technically Brody's spoils?

"Drink and eat to your hearts content," Brody said. "But be warned, the women are not for ye. They are under my protection. If anyone should touch, or attempt to speak to them, ye will suffer the consequences."

Many of the men grumbled their discontent, but none dared to say so to him openly.

She waited for him to introduce her to his men as his wife, but he did not. Instead, he dragged her to the kitchen door and tugged her through.

The servants, many of whom she recognized and a few that must have come with the Scots, worked to prepare food for the men. They stared at her, at Brody's hand on hers. They smirked. Still, he didn't declare her his wife, and those smirks said it all. They would think he was bedding her for sport. Heat fanned her face and made her throat tight.

But what did she care? They could all go to the devil. She'd done what she had to do to stay safe.

Let them think it. Even if it was a bruise to her ego. To be so used, even when she wasn't. Alas, what did their thoughts and opinions matter? Not much.

"Supper to the lady's chamber," he ordered, then dragged her into the great hall.

A man, as fearsome as Brody, stood near the hearth talking with several others. He was as tall as her new husband, his hair the color of oak bark, and his skin leathered from the sun. He flicked his gaze at Brody and grinned, the hair from his beard and mustache parting to show crooked but clean teeth.

"Marischal. What have ye here?"

Brody nodded to the man and pulled her forward. "Wallace, may I present Lady Guinevere, my new wife. And these are her ladies, under Keith protection."

Wallace turned his eyes to her and she felt like fainting.

William Wallace.

So this was the infamous leader of the Scottish rebellion. The very man who'd been plaguing the English for months. She'd heard so many stories about him. How he could cause a man to take his own life just by looking at him. That he'd simply walked onto Stirling Bridge and English soldiers had dove into the water for the want to get away from him. That he'd murdered the English lord in charge of the castle at Berwick-upon-Tweed with a soup spoon and that he was immortal, forged from the right hand of the devil himself.

He looked it. She believed it. There was a terrifying wildness in his eyes. A ruthless curve to his mouth. A sharpness to his features. A brutality about his body. A horror in the blood smeared on his plaid, soaked into the sleeves of his shirt.

What if he'd been the one to find her? Hadn't Brody said it was Wallace's idea to burn the kirk with the English knights inside? What would he have done to her?

Guinevere shuddered.

She didn't want him to know her name. Didn't want him to look at her. Lord, but she was desperate to get away. To run. Her limbs actually itched with the need for speed. When she didn't flee, her knees gave way to knocking together. Her hands trembled and a cold sweat broke out on her spine.

Brody glanced toward her, squinting his eyes as he assessed her. She worked to still her quaking body, somehow sensing from his gaze that strength was required right now.

That she was in a lion's den, and to show fear would mean certain death.

"Congratulations are in order, then. Ye have your castle. Ye have your bride. Ye have wenches. And"—Wallace raised a mug in his hand—"good French wine, too."

Brody nodded. "My thanks. Rest assured, I will not let the bonds of marriage be cause for me to shirk my duties. I have pledged my body and those of my men to the cause."

"Aye. Aye," Wallace said, his voice soft as his gaze perused her. "She is a beauty."

Brody's hand tightened on hers, until Guinevere realized it was her own grip that had intensified.

"If ye'll excuse me. I'd see her to her rooms and then I shall return to discuss our plans."

"Och, but tonight we shall forgo such. Tonight is for celebrating." Wallace wiggled his brows. "And I should say ye've got much celebrating to do." Wallace raised his glass.

The men around raised theirs and cheered as well.

"Shall we carry the two of ye upstairs?" Wallace asked.

"Nay," Brody said sternly.

Carry them? What could that mean?

And then she remembered her wedding in England. How the courtiers had followed them up the stairs at the de Ros castle. How they'd crowded around the bed, waiting in anticipation for her husband to climb in beside her. But then, they'd all left and the deed had never been done.

"Och, if ye would deprive the men of women, then at least allow them the privilege—"

"Nay." Brody's voice held an edge to it that she'd not heard before. He reached for the hilt of his sword, an act she knew all too well could end in bloodshed.

There was a tension between the two of them that grew. The two men stared at each other, silently assessing. Would they come to blows? Wallace was the clear leader of the rebellion and yet Brody was the Marischal of Scotland, a position that came with its own power.

With Brody's hand on his sword and Wallace flexing his hands at his side, she braced for the blows that were bound to come.

But then Wallace simply laughed and, standing beside her, she felt Brody's body release some, but not all, of the tension he held.

"Och, but ye are a right ornery bastard, Marischal. We'll all have to make do with our imaginations." He took a long drag on his cup, his eyes staring hard at her new husband.

"Aye." Brody nodded curtly, his hand dropping from his sword and returning loosely to his side. "I shall return shortly."

Wallace nodded, slugged back the contents of his mug and then returned his attention to the conversation he'd been having previously. It was only when they reached the stairs that she realized the trembling of her hands was not all her own. Brody shook slightly, too.

Just what were the repercussions for what he'd done? To not know them or understand them was dangerous even for her.

"Will you be punished?" she whispered.

"Nay."

"But, they all seem so—"

"Dinna concern yourself."

"But—"

Brody stopped walking abruptly and stared at her. "I said leave it alone. Ye will be safe. He can do nothing to me. I am not the only Scot to take an English bride."

He took the stairs two at a time and realizing she'd not the breadth of leg that he did, swiftly tugged her up into his arms and ran the rest of the way.

"Nay, the fourth floor," she murmured when he started off on the third.

Her ladies hurried behind, fear in their steps, in the small murmurings that grew fainter the quicker Brody went and the faster they tried to keep up. Noah kept his position at the rear of their line and, every so often, glanced behind him as if expecting men to follow.

Brody marched down the corridor and pushed open the broken door to her solar.

"This will not do. Ye'll not be safe with a broken door." He walked across the hall and pushed open another door. A chill draft swirled around them and he set her on the bed.

Her ladies and Noah filed in behind them.

"Supper shall be up shortly," he said grouchily. "Bar the door behind me. But make no mistake, ye will open it when I return."

And then he was gone, leaving Guinevere in a maelstrom of emotion.

She dropped into a chair by the hearth, staring into the barren grate. "What have I done?"

CHAPTER SEVEN

Brody didn't go immediately back to the great hall after washing the effects of battle from his body and changing into a clean leine shirt and plaid. Instead, he paced the corridor outside of the English wench's new chamber.

His wife.

An Englishwoman.

He was married.

Born and bred to hate him. Married to his enemy. Daughter of his enemy.

He rubbed at his forehead, feeling a headache coming on.

The servants brought up supper for the ladies and he inspected the meal being brought, making certain it wasn't inferior given the English's current situation. He was mildly surprised to find that the fare was well prepared and plentiful. Baked bread, a succulent stew, braised apples.

"Looks good," he said, eyeing the servants to see if they acted at all suspicious, perhaps they'd spit in the lassies' food. "Might I have a taste?"

"Of course, my laird." They did not appear to act awkward at all and easily offered him the fare. He tore a hunk of bread, dipping it in the stew and letting the savory flavors of the herbs, vegetables and meat melt on his tongue.

"Good," he murmured again.

"Her ladyship has always been good to us," the one holding the tray said.

Brody grunted, unsure what that was supposed to mean. Traveling with his camp was his own seneschal and cook from his castle in East Lothian, whom he'd asked to come and take charge at Dunnottar. He prayed they'd all work well together. "Go ahead. She is waiting."

Once they'd delivered the fare and left, Brody resumed his pacing.

"My laird," Noah said, his voice calm. "Would ye want me to stand sentry outside the door? Ye can go downstairs and get a bite to eat. Mayhap a dram of whisky."

Brody paused a minute, shook his head. "Nay, go on down. Ye've earned a night of revelry as much as any other."

Noah didn't budge.

"Suit yourself," Brody said, resuming his pacing.

Noah stood by the stairs, his dagger in hand picking at his nails, acting as though it were completely normal for Brody to be pacing outside of a woman's chamber like a man unsure of his own reality.

Stubborn arse.

As stubborn as himself. He was exhausted, in need of a stiff whisky and food. But he couldn't bring himself to descend the stairs. To listen to the jeers of the men about his wife, whether or not she'd been as cold and whining as they'd all heard English women were in bed.

The door opened as he passed it for the twentieth time and Guinevere stood there, small and enchanting. Her face still pale. Hair neatly done up. Her arm was outstretched and in her hand was a cup—possibly filled with poison.

"Drink," she said.

Brody stopped his pacing and shook his head, frowning. No words came to him, leaving him feeling addle-headed.

"'Tis not poisoned." She pushed it against his chest, quite forcibly, rolling her eyes. "You seem to need it."

He grunted, still incapable of words but plenty efficient at contemplations. A thousand of them, some good, some bad, some downright deplorable and plenty of them berating of himself, silently begging her to close the door.

Guinevere shrugged daintily, tipped the cup toward her lips and swallowed, a small shudder passing through her. "I'm not much of a whisky drinker, but de Ros was."

Brody stared at the small drop of whisky left on her lip, reaching to wipe at it with his thumb at the same time she licked the spot—swiping the pad of his finger with its heat.

His wife's cheeks flamed red and she bit the very spot he'd just touched. A more intimate moment he'd not experienced in so very long.

Brody cleared his throat, willing the blood that now led a torrent path to his groin to cease its quickened pace. "Your first husband."

81

She tilted her head to the side, perhaps dissecting his words in her mind, then nodded behind her. "This was his chamber."

The chit didn't appear to have much of a mourning air in regards to the loss of her husband. There was a sadness, even a fear. But he could sense no great loss. That, in and of itself, was odd.

Then again, if he'd been in her shoes, he'd not have enjoyed being married to an Englishman, either. Maybe the old saying was wrong. Maybe it was the Englishmen who were cold as fish, certainly just as slimy.

Brody reached for the cup and took a sip. The whisky was strong, bitter. Not the best, but did its job of taking the edge off his mood. Too much of it though and he'd be certain to have a nasty headache in the morning—and he'd likely forget his promise of waiting three months to bed her.

"That was kind of ye," he said suspiciously, handing her back the cup. "Why bother?"

"Hmm," she said. "Truly?"

"Aye." Now was when she'd admit being the only person alive who couldn't succumb to poison and that he'd downed it with a quick ease she'd not imagined.

"I did it because you're driving my ladies mad with your pacing. The whisky was a peace offering. And a bribe."

"A bribe?" He crossed his arms over his chest and raised a brow.

"Aye. I will refill your cup, even give you the bottle, if you would but leave us be."

Noah chuckled down at the end of the corridor and if Brody had not been in the presence of his bride, he would have slugged his cousin right in the jaw for his impertinence.

"The whisky was foul. If ye wish to bribe me, I can be persuaded in other ways." His gaze slid back to her lips.

The lass' face paled and her hand fluttered to her neck, drawing his stare to where a small pulse beat frantically. He wanted to touch the spot. To count how many times it beat in tune with his own. To touch his lip to the spot. To see if it sped up when he kissed her.

"What do you mean?" she asked innocently, though the way her gaze glided toward his mouth he knew she understood exactly what he meant. And damned if there wasn't a twinge of interest in her eyes, too.

"A kiss, *ma cherie*."

"You speak French?"

Brody chuckled. "We barbarians must know more languages than simply our own, how would ye put it, vulgar tongue?" His tone dropped with sarcasm, which was not lost on her given her frown.

"What is the translation of savage in your vulgar tongue?" Guinevere crossed her arms, leaning against the doorjamb, but the move only proved to pronounce the swell of her breasts and he couldn't stop staring.

As a result, the color in her cheeks heightened, and he bet the tiny pulse point, too. Damn, but maybe the whisky was stronger than he thought.

"*Sassenach*," he murmured, swaying closer toward her.

She didn't move and he found that to be very interesting. Was she growing used to him? Would she allow him to kiss her?

Zounds, but he wanted to.

"Well, *Sassenach*," she said. "I suggest you take the whisky over a kiss as at least it will bite less."

Noah was practically doubled over with laughter now, the heel of his boot hitting the floor. Brody ground his teeth, willing himself to not beat his cousin into a bloody pulp. Lord, but his frustration level was reaching beyond his coping point.

"*Sassenach* is what we Scots call ye English heathens," Brody said, frowning fiercely in hopes of intimidating her. "To call me such is a grave insult."

"Oh, truly?" There she shrugged again. The lass did not seem in the least bit afraid of him. "The sound of it seemed much more fitting to someone of your ilk."

Her lack of fear fascinated him. She had been more cautious before he'd married her. Perhaps that was a mistake. Mayhap when he'd pledged his protection she'd taken that as meaning he'd not harm her. Well, he would bloody well show her that he was to be feared. Respected.

She'd been bloody terrified of Wallace. Had even sought comfort from Brody, holding tight to his hand. Brody had liked that. He'd liked providing her with the comfort she sought—as much as it irritated him, too. All the same, he couldn't have her thinking that now that they were married she could walk all over him, fear every Scot but him. Wasn't that the way of things? That a wife should fear and respect her husband? Well, he didn't really know, but it sounded right.

Brody leaned close, his face only inches from hers. "Just because we've exchanged vows does not mean I'll not hesitate to take ye over my knee. A husband deserves respect. He demands it."

Guinevere's lips pressed in on themselves, as though she were trying to frown in order to hide her laughter.

"Ye are a saucy wench, are ye not?" He wasn't truly asking, only realizing it, perhaps a bit too late. "Why are ye not afraid of me?"

"You seem a man who takes pride in ownership," she replied tartly, her gaze never wavering from his.

Brody crossed his arms over his chest, trying to appear bigger. "I do."

"And you've made it clear I am to be your property." With each word, her brows rose higher toward her hairline as if willing him to understand her.

"I have."

Now she smiled, proud of herself for having figured something out that she'd not shared with him. "Then you'd not damage your property."

Ah, she'd tried to trap him with his own words. "I might make it sting a bit." Brody's voice was low and he hoped a little menacing. "Dinna take my offer of protection, my kindness toward your wishes as a weakness, lass."

Guinevere sucked in a gasp. Her hand jerked out, but she pulled it back swiftly, before it connected with him. "You don't have to be such a boar."

A boar? Was she truly comparing him to a wild animal? Even more shocking, was she going to hit him?

Brody sucked his teeth and replied crudely, "If I'm a boar, then I'd not have agreed to keep my tusk from piercing your flesh."

That had her backing up, her hand over her lips, all sense of hostility evaporated in her offense. But Brody wasn't going to let her disappear into her chamber, not enough to slam the door in his face.

He snaked out his arm and wrapped it around her waist, tugging her closer.

"Please," she whimpered, fear in her eyes. "You promised."

That was what he'd been going for—fear. But seeing it in her eyes made him sick to his stomach. That wasn't who he was. That wasn't what he wanted from her.

He let go, taking a wide step back. "Curb your venom, mistress," he said slowly, jabbing his cup toward her. "I'm a man of honor."

With a trembling hand, she took his cup. She nodded enough that her head bobbed, giving off the affect that she was more convincing herself than agreeing with him.

"Bar the door. Let no one in." Brody took another long look at her before turning on his heel, leaving her gaping after him.

Noah had regained his sense, no laughter on his lips now. He followed behind Brody's pounding steps, down the circular stairs and back to the great hall.

The men had grown more rowdy, with drinks in hand and food piled on the long trestle tables, eyes red, skin flushed. Several serving wenches lounged with the men, kissing them and whispering in their ears. At least the English wenches upstairs had been forgotten. For now.

Brody found Wallace sitting at the dais table with several of his men, two chairs left empty in the center.

"Come join us!" Wallace shouted. "We've saved ye a seat at the head, of course, since ye are the new master here. Though we didna expect to see ye so soon."

Brody and Noah approached the table, the former forcing out a laugh.

"A timid bride, English at that, does not give a man pause to last for long."

The men let out a loud cheer with that, and though Brody had done so for that reaction, his own derision toward Guinevere left him feeling unsettled.

"Sit with me," he said to his cousin.

Noah sat quietly beside him, the both of them uneasy.

This was the part that Brody hated the most in regards to their situation. Wallace and he were friends. They were partners. And he felt now a wedge had been driven between them that would be hard to smooth out.

They filled their plates and Brody drained his glass of wine before the servant could step away, and so it was refilled quickly. His body had warmed, growing numb around the edges with drink.

He and Noah sat in silence through the meal, responding when spoken to only, but offering up nothing else to the conversation. Every bite he put in his mouth, despite its delicious scent, left no taste on his tongue. Brody was still reeling about the women upstairs, still felt ill about the dead English in the kirk. He knew it would be up to him to see the bones buried, to begin rebuilding, to form some sort of relationship with his new bride. After all, Dunnottar was now his and so was she.

Wallace leaned toward him. "I'm afraid ye've got more work then ye realized."

Brody grunted, assuming Wallace meant his wife.

"The kirk fire leapt, catching fire to several of the out buildings and part of the wall which they leaned up against has collapsed." Wallace tore a large bite out of his bread.

So, his leader would not mention his wife. Brody was relieved, if a little uneasy. He nodded to Wallace. "I'll see the work begins immediately."

"Good. Dunnottar has the ability to be one of the most fortified castles in the Highlands. I'm certain de Brus will want to make a base here at some point." Wallace took a long sip of his ale. "We'll be leaving in the morning," he said, "after the men help ye clean up the kirk."

The bodies is what he meant, and Brody was glad that the Guardian seemed to finally develop some sort of compassion, even if the men burned alive were their enemies.

No quarter. That was their order. Brody begged forgiveness from the heavens, for they'd no way to know if the kirk had only been filled with English soldiers or more casualties of war.

"Where are ye headed?" Brody asked.

"South, likely toward the border. I've a mind to invade England." Wallace grinned like a man with his eye on a treasure no one had yet discovered. "Give Longshanks a taste of what he's been dealing us."

Invading England would be dangerous. Aye, for certes many Scots had conducted border raids. For centuries, the castle at Berwick-upon-Tweed had traded hands. But Wallace wasn't talking about a raid, nay, invasion. And if any man was to be successful at invading England, it would be Wallace.

"I've more men waiting for me at Ettrick Forest. They are building weapons. Fashioning armor. Gathering supplies. They'll be ready when I arrive."

Ettrick Forest, Wallace's base for all his military operations.

"I will come as soon as I can. Take some of my men with ye."

Wallace nodded. "Ye've two thousand strong. How many can ye part with?"

"Take fifteen hundred. Five hundred here should be enough to assist with fortifications and then we will follow in perhaps a month's time."

"We will celebrate our many victories, my friend," Wallace said. "England has not a hint of what is coming for them."

"Och, Wallace, but I think they do, and they're likely pissing themselves over it. Every one of them wondering if ye'll skin them alive like Cressingham, or burn them in blazing hell fires." Brody scrubbed his hand over his face. "Nay, they are not without an inclination. Ye've made a name for yourself. They fear ye. Let them fear ye as we have feared Longshanks." Brody raised his glass high. "To Wallace!"

The men at the trestle tables and those spilling out into the courtyard and beyond. raised their glasses and shouted the same.

Wallace, in turn, raised his glass and bellowed, "To Scotland! To freedom!"

Freedom. That was the root of it all. To be brought out from under the thumb of the English. To have the right to choose their own leader. To not be fearful that their noblemen would be bought off by Longshanks, to betray their own kin.

"To freedom!"

CHAPTER EIGHT

Guinevere lay awake most of the night, only dozing here and there, and jerking awake at any sudden movement or sound.

Sleeping in de Ros' bed was unnerving. She prayed for his soul, that he was at peace, for however tormented he'd been in life. The year they'd been married, she'd never grown close to him. He'd not allowed it. Not been interested. She was a means to an end—or rather a way up, a new beginning, that didn't necessarily have to involve her.

But beyond sleeping in his bed, she'd been worried throughout the night that Brody would go back on his promise of not consummating their marriage. That he would come to her in a drunken, savage stupor, force himself on her.

Trying to prove something to her, to himself, to the men downstairs.

From below stairs, raucous laughter, shouts and merriment reverberated. Surely he was participating in the merriment. The celebration of victory. The gaiety of having taken lives and not lost their own. Of having conquered the castle and gotten himself a bride.

But he never came.

There was never any twist of the door handle.

No call from him on the other side.

He left her alone.

And perhaps what was most disturbing of all—she'd not actually gotten the impression from him that he would do that. As much bluster as he gave her, she could sense there was a deep wound within him, that he was a good man despite his blood.

Just before dawn, she fell asleep. A hard and deep, dreamless sleep.

"My lady." Elinor stroked her shoulder and Guinevere rolled over. "Wake.

"Nay." She swatted her maid's hand away.

Elinor shook her shoulder a little more forcefully then. "Please, you must wake."

Guinevere reluctantly sat up straight, eyes burning from lack of sleep. Her head pounded and when she took in the sight of de Ros' room, all that had happened the day before came tunneling back. All three of her maids stood in the chamber, dressed, hair plaited, and on the table in the corner were freshly baked scones, stewed apples and honeyed porridge.

"The men, they are preparing to leave," Abigail murmured.

"Leave?" Guinevere tossed back her blankets and ran toward the window, recalling as she reached it that the master's chamber faced the sea rather than the bailey below. Odd, really, since a master should want to see who approached the castle, unless of course, it was because the threat came more from the sea. She didn't care to deliberate on it any further.

She pulled on her robe and stormed, barefoot, across the hallway, shoving aside the broken door to her chamber, hopping around the fallen wardrobe and then rushing to the window.

Sure enough, in the bailey below, Scottish warriors were readying their horses. Most of them looked to have cleaned themselves up after battle, but not all of them. She supposed some of the men truly were savages—not any different than some of the English knights that had ridden in de Ros' camp.

But more than that, she saw many men pulling wagons of burnt wood... and was that a... skull? Their faces were covered in ash and grime, their once creamy linen shirts covered in black streaks.

They were intently cleaning the church. Taking the bones and debris through the gate. Would they bury them or offer the remains up to the fairies of the glen? Their faces were grim and she could see tear stains through their sooty cheeks on several. It was... heart wrenching and eye opening. As brutal as their attack had been, these men took death seriously.

"I need to get dressed," she murmured.

"But your breakfast," Elinor urged. "You barely touched your dinner last eve. You must eat. You must remain strong."

Guinevere tugged at the long rope of her braided hair. "How can I eat when they are be clearing the ashes of our countrymen? I should be praying or giving my food to a much hungrier child. Or even helping to clear the rubble."

Elinor bit her lip, placed a hand on Guinevere's shoulder. "Please. Don't go down there."

"Give me a good reason not to." Guinevere despised the harsh tone in her voice, but she couldn't help it. The events of the day before, the last year were a waking nightmare.

Elinor's eyes shifted and she stepped closer, lowering her voice. "I spoke with Sir Noah this morning."

Sir Noah... Right. "The Marischal's cousin."

"Aye, your *husband's* cousin." Elinor gave her a look that said she'd better accept it sooner or later.

Guinevere accepted it. More so than anyone realized. She was forever linked to this man. Well, until he passed on like her first husband, or she found a way to escape, which seemed impossible when every inch of ground surrounding the castle was occupied by a warrior. "Tell me what he said."

"The men are grumpy. Their heads pound from too much drink. Wallace's men and three-quarters of the Keith men will leave as soon as they've cleaned out the church. Wait until then, when you're less likely to..." Elinor's voice trailed off, but Guinevere knew what she was getting at. Wait until it was less likely she'd be attacked by one of the thousands of men below.

She swallowed around the bitterness of that reality. "And my... husband?"

93

"He and the rest of his men will remain here for a time to repair the wall and other destroyed buildings."

"The kirk?"

"They will rebuild it and make it grander."

Guinevere crossed herself. "Am I doomed to walk eternity in Purgatory for having married my enemy? For having married the man partially responsible for de Ros' demise?"

"Don't think like that, my lady. There is still time to redeem him. And, you and I both know de Ros was no innocent. He killed many of the men who built the original kirk. He was already doomed."

Guinevere nodded. She knew what Elinor said was true. But even truths had the power to make one doubt.

She thought about the warrior she'd married. His stormy, gray eyes, the pain that he hid so well. She recalled her interaction with him in the corridor the night before. Aye, her new husband was handsome, and when he'd asked for a kiss as payment, part of her had leapt at the chance to feel his lips on hers again, but the other part of her... That part had been wary of the brooding darkness that simmered just beneath the surface of his armor. He was as a man disturbed. A man with many secrets. "I do not think I can redeem him." A swift wind blew in through the window, rustling the hem of her robe and nightrail as if in agreement. "He is filled with torment that only he can liberate himself from." She sighed. "I had hoped he'd be leaving with the men, that I might have a chance to escape."

"Escape?" Elinor shook her head. "Do you know who you married?"

Guinevere narrowed her eyes and snapped, "Well, obviously, you do, perhaps you'd best inform me."

"I am Brody Keith, Earl Marischal of Scotland."

Guinevere sucked in her breath and whirled, crossing her arms over herself. " I know who you are. I was being sarcastic."

Brody raised his brows, studying her as though he wanted to make sure she'd not bite his head off. Well, she might.

"I'm not dressed. You need to leave."

"Ye look to be clothed to me, though I'd not suggest ye went outside like that."

"I'm not." She jutted her chin forward, wrapping her robe tighter. "What do you want?"

He jerked his head at Elinor, who complied entirely too quickly for Guinevere's liking, as she scurried from the room.

"I came to see how ye slept."

"Why should you care how I slept?" She backed up as he walked forward. She was feeling very much like prey being stalked by a hunter.

"Ye're my wife. Am I not supposed to care about such things?"

"Have you been married before?" she asked.

"Nay."

Aha! Something she was held superior. "Well, I have, and my husband, whom you have murdered, did not ask such things."

Brody made a *tsking* sound and came even closer, fingering the curtains on the bed she'd slept in every night except last. "For one thing, *iasg beag,* I did not murder your husband. For another, did it ever occur to ye that perhaps ye should have asked?"

Guinevere swallowed around the lump forming in her throat. "What?"

95

He cocked his head at her, his gray eyes assessing. "To which statement are ye referring?"

She straightened her shoulders, hating that the closer he got, the more her mind lost its sense and her skin heated, as though her body remembered the possessive way he'd gripped her hip, the expert stroking of his tongue on her lips. "You may not have personally caused his death, but you were a part of the siege. In fact, you now claim this castle and its lands as your own. I do hold you responsible for his death."

"I concede." He bowed before her. "And I beg your forgiveness. For if I'd known the plan from the beginning, I would have altered it."

"What?" Brody continued to baffle her. He was not saying the things she expected him to. Not responding in the way she was prepared. It was confusing. And wrong. She liked it better when he growled. When she could snap back at him.

"Lass, if ye continue to question my words, I might be moved to think ye were daft."

Guinevere pressed her lips together, irritated that he should be so full of wit and so quick with his words when everything he said to her addled her brain. Maybe she was daft. Perhaps all that had happened had finally broken her.

"For another thing," she continued, choosing to ignore him, "It is impolite for you to inquire about my day or night." She was, of course, making this up, but what would he know? He was a heathen, barbarian, savage. "For another, we should not care about what one another does during the day, only that we each remain loyal to the other."

Brody chuckled. "How verra odd, *iasg beag.*"

"What does that mean? *Ee-ask-bec*?"

Brody's grin widened at her choppy pronunciation of his language.

"It means…" His eyes danced with mirth. "*My wife*."

"Hmm." Guinevere narrowed her eyes. She might not have known him long, but she already knew he liked to tease her, and that look he had in his eye had certainly been full of jest. "Is this like when you said *Sassenach* means barbarian?"

His head tilted back and he belted out a laugh that shook the rafters. How out of place it seemed, and yet the sound made her want to laugh. Made her want to dance around to the music of happiness. But she was a lady, and trying to prove a point besides, so she remained stoic and acerbic.

"Aye. Just like that, lass."

Drat, he wasn't going to tell her the true meaning. She supposed she'd not know the true meaning of his words just yet and they'd likely drive her crazy every time he said them.

Guinevere studied her new husband, determined not to like him but finding him too charming to resist. If only he could just be the brooding boar he was sometimes and not the flirt he seemed to be right now. The fact that the dark side of him only reared occasionally meant that it wasn't the true him. Well, not in a permanent sense of the word.

Brody Keith was a man with a painful past, she decided. Not unlike many she'd met. How could he not be? His country was besieged by war. His previous king abdicated and was now a prisoner at the Tower of London. His desired king considered a rebel.

Beyond his country's torment, what had he seen?

Zounds, but why did she care?

That was another rule she should tell him—neither of them should be concerned with the other's feelings.

The man had stormed her castle, ripped her world apart and then married her. She should be running for her life.

But she wasn't.

In fact, he didn't scare her at all. A notion that was almost as disturbing as the fact that she kind of liked him.

Heavens, but she needed some air. Her old chamber was suddenly stifling, the walls closing in on her.

"Will you have someone fix this door?" She fanned her hand toward the crumbling wood.

"Och, aye, lass. I'll fix it myself. And my apologies for having stormed through it to begin with."

"Let us be honest with each other, Brody," she said, narrowing her eyes. "For we are joined now in a union, however unholy. I will not pretend you are my knight in shining armor, come to rescue me, and you do not pretend that I am your loving wife whom you cherish and dote on."

Brody looked taken aback by her words. His eyes widened and his lips slackened.

She straightened, forging ahead. "And please, do not fix this door yourself. Have one of your men do it. I do not need another thing in which I should feel obliged to you for."

"Obliged?" Brody nearly choked on the word. "Ye're a cold woman, Guinevere. Dinna think for a minute that I came to Dunnottar with the intent to marry. Dinna flatter yourself that the moment I saw ye I fell head over heels. Dinna think I wished to sweep ye off your feet and carry ye away into the sunset like ye fanciful women like to think. If anything, I wanted to wrench ye over my knee and slap your arse until it was a red as a rose, and then I wanted to run. I wanted to get as far away from ye as possible. Do ye think it odd that a man, thirty and two, would not have begotten a wife as of yet?" He stepped closer, invading her space and making it hard for her to breathe. She'd not seen so much passion, so much of himself since he'd kissed her. "Do ye think a hot-blooded man such as myself would agree not to take what was rightfully mine for three months, except out of the hope that by pleasing my wife, I could make a life that wasn't so utterly unpleasant?"

Now it was her turn to be speechless. Guinevere swallowed, but her throat was so incredibly tight.

"I married ye to keep ye from being raped, repeatedly, and then discarded. I married ye so ye could keep whatever virtue ye had left after being married to an English bastard. And all I asked from ye in return was respect and obedience. What did I get instead? A cold wench with nettles for a tongue."

Guinevere blanched. He'd not been so blunt with her before. The word rape resounded in her mind.

She'd had an idea that he'd not wanted her for a wife, but... she'd not thought about it in such finite detail. That he'd not only not wanted her to be his wife, he'd not wanted a wife at all. That he'd married her out of obligation to keep her safe and put his own life on the life by doing so.

Lord, but she could barely breathe. She'd been so selfish to think only of herself, that perhaps his life was no longer going the way it was planned. That because of chivalry and honor, he'd married her to keep her from being abused. Repeatedly. What did he gain from marrying her? Nothing. She wouldn't even let him bed her. And she wouldn't, simply out of guilt, either.

Her new husband, bristling, wasn't done yet.

"Ye're lucky it was me that followed ye to the beach. Ye're lucky it was me that de Brus chose as the new master of this place."

She sucked in a ragged breath. "You're right."

"What?"

"I should be grateful that ye kept me from such a fate. I should be grateful that I am still alive and that I wasn't burned in that church." Oh dear heavens, why were tears stinging her eyes? "I should be grateful for so many things. But I'm not." Nay! That was not what she wanted to say! She wanted to be complacent, to get him to leave her in peace, so that he wouldn't suspect when she set them both free. But the stubborn, fiery side of her fought back, even against his gallantry.

"I didna expect anything less than acid from ye." His stormy eyes searched hers, filled with anger, frustration.

"I didn't want to come here to Scotland anymore than you wanted to take me to wife. So we're even, savage."

Brody gritted his teeth, the scraping sound piercing her ears. "I am not a savage." His words were slow, ground out of his mouth to a fine powder.

He wasn't. She knew that. He'd proved that enough. He might look the part but he had more manners than most of the Englishmen she'd ever met.

Guinevere looked toward the ground. At his dusty black leather boots that were inches from her bare toes.

"Nay, you're not," she whispered.

Brody skimmed his fingers beneath her chin, urging her to look up. And when she did, she wished she hadn't. There was pity in his eyes.

"Ye're not as cold as ye were yesterday."

"I feel colder inside," she whispered.

"I know not the thoughts that are going through your mind," he said. "Nor, can I take back what has happened. But I can give ye a promise, lass. I will protect ye. I will try to make ye happy."

"But, why?"

"Because there are worse things out there, Guinevere. There are far worse things."

CHAPTER NINE

Confession had been on the tip of his tongue.

Every dark thought that ran rampant in his mind had nearly spilled in a vast deluge of blackness. Saints, but her eyes were watering, on the brink of tears, and the way she was looking up at him now was as though he held the key to some mysterious lock.

He clamped his mouth closed, forcing back the verbal torrents that desperately wanted to be set free. Och, but he longed to get it off his chest. But there was always some chain pulling the truth of his pain back. How could he admit to the woman he'd just promised to protect that he'd not even been able to protect his own family?

Nay. What he'd said was enough already.

That was as far as he was willing to go. As much as he would say. She knew the truth of her situation, the truth of any female's plight in war times. He needn't tell her about Johanna. Needn't reveal such details.

Guinevere might be brave, might pretend to be as tough as iron, but even the strongest metal had a weak point.

Before he could stop himself, Brody reached forward, his arm circling her shoulders. He tugged her to him. Pressing her tear-stained cheeks to his chest, his chin resting on her head. The thinness of her nightrail left little the imagination, but somehow his body knew now was not the time to react to her in a sensual way—though he did appreciate every curve.

"Dinna cry," he murmured, swaying gently. He patted her back, stroked her hair and reflexively kissed her brow.

"I don't know why I am," she said, shaking her head against his chest. "I rarely cry."

For some reason, judging from his encounters with her in the past two days, he believed that.

Brody couldn't offer her a reason why she cried now, because truth be told, he didn't know. Living with his sisters, he'd seen them wail about the most trivial things to the most devastating. Women cried. That was a fact. He simply thought they all cried for no reason, or any reason. The fact that this one was bringing it up at all was awkward to him, and yet enlightening.

He awkwardly patted her back, feeling as though his large hands were pounding out the tears, so he forced himself to stop.

They stood still for several long moments, the front of his leine growing wet, until her sobs subsided and she gently pushed him away.

Her gaze on the floor, Guinevere said, "My thanks for allowing me a moment to blubber." She discreetly wiped at her tears. "I promise I'll not allow myself to come undone like that again." Her hands waved in the air and she glanced toward the ceiling. "There's just been... so much that's happened. I'm afraid I was overwhelmed."

"Ye need not apologize for it, lass." Brody grabbed hold of one of her waving hands and brought it to his lips. She smelled sweet, like rays of sunshine on a blustery day. "As your husband, 'tis my duty to comfort ye."

Her red-rimmed blue-green eyes met his, filled with uncertainty and, perhaps, a spark of something more like hope. "I'm not certain that is one of your duties."

Again she went with her English customs. Brody shook his head. "'Haps not for a *Sassenach*, but for me, it is."

She smiled tentatively, a jovial light returning somewhat to her eyes. "You're sweet for a barbarian."

Brody grinned. "And ye're not as frosty as I'd assumed a *Sassenach* wench to be."

"If it's all the same, perhaps we'd best get a list together of expectations as I'm uncertain what you might expect of me."

"I told ye, I only want for ye to respect me, to honor me, to trust me, to obey."

She chewed her lip, giving him a look that said she wasn't certain she could comply or agree. Brody just shook his head, truly not expecting anything less or more of her. She was simply herself, and as ornery and stubborn as she was, he was fascinated by her.

Brody walked her back across the hall to her chamber where her ladies waited with wide eyes, tugging her into their protective fold.

"Thank you, my laird," she whispered as the door was slowly closed.

"Ye're more than welcome, *iasg beag*."

Brody stared at the closed door, his mind working faster than he could fully comprehend. What had just happened? Had they just opened up to each other? Even if only slightly? He shook his head. How fascinating and yet... disconcerting. He needed a distraction. And quick. Else he knock on the door and beg her to let him sit at her feet while she patted his hair like a dog.

Whirling toward the stairs, he descended with speed and sailed into the bailey in search of Wallace to discuss the plans for restoration.

By the time the evening rolled around, Brody was exhausted. He took his supper in his new study and tried to make sense of the ledgers and maps of the holding. At some point, he'd have to make a progress of the perimeter, and that had him wondering if Guinevere had ever done so. Most likely not.

The English had sailed in, taken over the castle and then sat there, using it as a base with which to fight those in the north. Making any sort of progress would have been asking for trouble.

Bastards.

Brody sat back in his chair, swiping his hand over the sweat gathered on his forehead. With a thousand men working on the kirk that morning, the debris had been quickly cleaned up. The bodies were buried and the Keith chaplain had consecrated the earth and given the last rights to the English buried in the woods beyond the cliffs.

Wallace and fifty-five hundred men had marched out, taking with them many of the supplies on hand. With winter looming, there was also the incoming weather and being stranded to contend with. The granary stores were low from the English before them and now with the Scottish army needing to be resupplied. Winter would be tight if they didn't do something about it soon. He could use extra coin from his own coffers to purchase supplies and ask his seneschal, Artair, if there was enough extra in his own stores even to restock.

Already, he'd had messages sent out to the nearby villages to come and pay homage to him in two days' time. At that time, he'd be assessing taxation and hearing any grievances. 'Twas best to get all of that handled quickly as he planned to return to join Wallace at the border once more.

The Keith name carried a lot of weight and demanded respect. Brody demanded it and received it easily. He expected the people of Dunnottar would be beyond thrilled to have a Scot as their leader once more, and to know that he was rebuilding the kirk, too, and that any of the men of the church who wished to return would always be welcomed by him.

He was considering leaving Noah here in charge while he was away, but his cousin would probably balk at the prospect. Noah wanted to make a name for himself in battle. But there was also his betrothal to the Oliphant lass to consider. Her father had been captured at the Battle of Dunbar, the very same one that had taken his sister's and father's lives, and was now being held prisoner in England.

Noah wanted to help his intended. To prove that he was worthy of her, by helping to free her father. Noah wanted to be a hero and Brody couldn't fault him for that. All the same, Noah would not argue if Brody insisted, his first duty being to his clan, especially since he was the only heir to Brody's title, lands and fortune, at the moment.

On that same note, Brody didn't want to push his cousin into the life he'd forged for himself, one in which love and friendship never before played a part. He wasn't a family man by nature and he wasn't certain he could even fake it.

Brody pushed away from the desk and poured himself some whisky, swishing it around in his mouth and then pouring another dram. The drink calmed his racing thoughts enough that he was able to get back to work reading through various missives that the English bastard had in his possession. A gold mine, really. Brody now had at his disposal the plans the English had for the north. Which general was in charge of which plot of land. Possible dates for meetings. Who the English wanted to imprison and which castles were considered contenders for seizing.

One missive in particular caught his eye. It was from a French ambassador stating that the French king was being persuaded to side with the English, rescinding his alliance with the Scots.

"Bloody hell," Brody breathed out. They'd been counting on a continued alliance.

With his candle already burning low, Brody lit another and went to work penning missive after missive. One to de Brus, one to Wallace and one to Andrew Murray. All of them needed to be made aware of the impending French duplicity.

In the wee hours of the morning, Noah knocked at the door, looking like he hadn't much sleep either.

"Have ye been up all night?"

Brody nodded, rolling his missives and sealing them with wax.

"We may soon have more to fear than the English."

"Who?"

"There's a missive here from the French ambassador to Baron de Ros that states he should soon be hearing from the French king about an alliance."

"King Philip has always been a bastard. Dangling the carrot of his help only to snatch it back when we need it most," Noah muttered.

"Aye, but now he'll be aiding Longshanks and we'll not even be getting the chance to snatch the carrot."

"As it happens, King Philip's dauphine is up for grabs—Isabella. She is to be betrothed to Longshanks' son, Edward."

Noah grunted. "If only we had someone whom Philip could give his daughter."

"With Robert de Brus newly married, the only other option would be Wallace or Andrew," Brody mused. "Neither of whom Philip would consider, I'm certain, given their less than royal bloodlines."

"Damn." Noah rubbed his chin. "Perhaps a promise of heirs in the de Brus line to come?"

"'Tis unlikely that will work and so we are thwarted." Brody dragged his hand through his hair. "I need to see these missives off. I've a feeling I willna be here as long as I planned."

"Let me know what ye need of me, cousin."

Brody nodded. "I know ye want to get back to the border."

Noah shifted his stance. "Aye, cousin. I want to invade England with Wallace. 'Haps find where they've imprisoned Saundra's father and bring him back to Scotland."

Brody pursed his lips, then smiled. "Ye'd be the hero for her."

"Just as ye were the hero for your wife."

Brody almost choked, half wondering if he'd heard him correctly. "I do not think they are the same."

Noah shrugged. "They are both threatened by the English."

"My wife *is* English," Brody pointed out.

Noah grinned, letting out a soft chuckle. "Not anymore."

Brody pictured the obstinate turn of her lips, the way she crossed her arms delicately, yet full of stubbornness, across her chest. "I dinna think she'll agree with ye."

"Bah." Noah chuckled and waved away the notion. "Will ye rest? Ye look like hell."

"I'll rest when I'm dead. No time for such luxuries now. Come, I must see that they've started fortifications on the wall that crumbled."

Noah followed Brody out to the bailey. He sent three riders with the various missives to be delivered and then approached the wall. There had been several outbuildings along the wall that burned to the ground. A small group of men gathered around him.

"A fletcher, a blacksmith and a tanner," Brody mused. "Where are they?"

He turned to the various men who'd come to observe the damage. One man stepped forward, his mouth drawn down in dejection. How many awful things had this man witnessed before his shop was burned to the soil?

109

"I am Angus, the blacksmith. Fergus, the fletcher was murdered by the English last year, they'd brought their own man with them. And our tanner is ill, laid up at home this last week."

"Has a healer been to see him?"

"Aye, my laird. Says its just an ague that will heal in time."

"That is good to know. We'll rebuild," Brody said, gazing over the charred remains. Piles of charred wood, scraps of metal, a flap of tanned leather, burned and curling at the corners. "Dunnottar will thrive, ye have my word."

The men nodded and Brody gave directions on how to fortify the wall with stone and mortar so that it wouldn't so easily burn the next time around—then crossed himself there was never such another time. The outbuildings would be cleaned up and then rebuilt, but this time, several feet away from the wall rather than backing to it.

Since he and Wallace had been able to scale the cliff and easily drop down on the men at the gate, the walls were to be built higher there, crenellated, with a wooden walkway that could be easily removed should it seem a siege was imminent.

"Is that the English vessel?" Brody asked an elder clansman, pointing out to the sea where a ship was anchored. Its sails had been tied, the masts stabbing starkly toward the sky. An empty, ghostlike vessel. Even from here he could see the English flag had faded and grown limp, laying flat to the mast rather than waving in the wind.

"Aye, my laird. They couldn't bring it close enough because of the shoals and rock that'll easily damage a ship.

The *Sassenachs* took turns manning their ship until a month ago."

"And what happened a month ago?"

"Smallpox, or some such. Took the crew out and de Ros said that any who boarded would become ill with it. He was biding his time, waiting the requisite quarantine time."

Brody grunted. "Which is?"

"I've not a clue, my laird, but seems the time has passed now."

Brody wasn't going to take any chances. He'd check with a healer before sending anyone out to investigate.

"The bodies are still aboard?"

The man shook his head.

"Where are they?"

"Dumped at sea or they jumped."

"And the disease never spread to the castle?"

"Nay, my laird. De Ros might have been a bastard, but he was cautious."

"Not cautious enough." Brody thanked the elder for his help and then turned back to his men. They were working hard to clear away the damage of the wall and outbuildings, salvaging anything they could reuse or that wasn't completely damaged.

His cook, Mrs. Donald, from East Lothian, a nervous-looking elderly woman with graying hair, approached. She dipped a quick curtsy. "My laird."

"Aye?"

"Lady Guinevere is asking if she may be allowed to plan the meals for the men."

"Is that not her duty?" Brody asked with a raised brow. What kind of trouble was the woman causing now?

111

"Aye, but she wasn't certain if it was one ye wished her to complete, something about what is custom."

Brody frowned. Why did his wife insist that their ways of life were so very different? He couldn't imagine that they were so different inside a marriage and a castle, even if the way they fought on the field of battle was.

"Please inform my wife that her duties as Mistress of Dunnottar should remain as they were before."

The woman shifted her eyes, chewed on her lip and looked altogether too uncomfortable for Brody's peace of mind.

"What is it?" he asked.

"'Tis nothing, my laird. I shall tell her."

Brody gritted his teeth and rather than argue with the old woman, he nodded curtly. "Starting with my permission to plan the meals."

"Aye, my laird." She curtsied, backing away from him. "Thank ye, my laird."

If he could just get a peek inside his wife's mind, it may clear up a whole lot of confusion on his part. Alas, he supposed he'd continue to be left in the dark.

There was entirely too much to be done with the castle to worry over it now. Perhaps if he'd not fallen asleep by the evening meal, he'd ask her to explain herself, but his patience was already wearing thin and it seemed that every encounter he had with her either made him want to wring her slender neck, or kiss her until she they were both panting for more—which they couldn't because, like an idiot, he'd agreed not to bed her for three bloody months.

CHAPTER TEN

Guinevere simmered as she stared at the broken wooden door. Beside her were planks of board, iron nails and a hammer.

"Why would he think you should rebuild the door?" Abigail asked, chewing on her nail and bending to inspect the wooden planks, pinching the edges as though they were dirty laundry.

Guinevere knew exactly why her new brooding husband would make such an order—because she'd told him she didn't want *him* to do it. Oh, she could call to mind vividly the bitter words she'd said and this was how he'd punish her! If she didn't want him to do it, what better way to retaliate than to tell her to see the fixing of the door done herself.

113

Well, she was going to build the best darn door anyone had ever seen! Brody would be so impressed, he'd have to stuff his boot far down his throat in order to contain himself.

"Are you certain Mrs. Donald said he wanted you to build the door?"

Guinevere nodded, hands on her hips as she examined the broken wood that hung awkwardly on the hinges. "Aye. I went to the kitchen to discuss the noon meal and she said she'd have to check with *the master* first." She frowned, tapping her chin. "She never refers to him as my husband, and even though he's insisting I choose his meals, she never listens to what I have to say. Huh. No matter, that will all get sorted in time. As I was saying, when she came back she said he did not want me choosing what he would eat any longer. That only a Scot should be choosing what a Scot should eat and that, instead, I should put myself to good use and fix this door."

Saints, but her blood was boiling. How dare he? To say only a Scot should be choosing what a Scot should eat... Guinevere bit the tip of her tongue before something unladylike escaped. Aye, she'd been initially brought to Dunnottar for nefarious purposes, but she'd done her best to keep the people here happy. To not insist too harshly that they treat her as an Englishwoman. Why was Mrs. Donald giving her such a hard time? Mayhap it was only because the woman didn't know her. She didn't realize that Guinevere was different than other English ladies perhaps.

Mrs. Donald was relatively new to the castle. She'd come with the Wallace and Brody and had swiftly taken control of the kitchen from the staff who'd been here before, claiming to have worked for Brody for years and knowing the exact way in which he wanted things done. Eager to please their new master, everyone had folded with ease into Mrs. Donald's rather gnarled and unkind hands.

"It just seems so odd," Abigail muttered, picking up a nail and testing the sharpness on the tip of her finger.

Claudia had barely spoken since the day before and had been resting all morning with a headache. Guinevere was starting to getting worried. Claudia didn't have the best disposition and was prone to bouts of melancholy and worry. Especially since they'd come to Scotland. If she had the opportunity to send Claudia home, she was going to, and hopefully that opportunity would present itself soon. Brody had said her ladies could return, but he'd yet to make good on his word. Granted, they had a lot going on at the current moment and who would readily agree to escort two very uptight English ladies back to England? Guinevere honestly couldn't see any of the men volunteering for the job.

"I will find out if this is the case, or if Mrs. Donald is simply playing games with you." Elinor stood tall. "If I may be so bold as to suggest you not pick up a single nail until I return."

Guinevere let out a long sigh, resting her hands on her hips. "The truth is, Elinor, I *want* to fix this door. To prove to Brody Keith, or Mrs. Donald, that I'm not as useless and weak as I know he thinks I am. This is a test. He probably expects me to come storming into the bailey demanding that someone else fix the door. But I refuse. I will not bend to his childish games. And if Mrs. Donald is behind it, well, then soon her attempts to make me look less in my husband's eyes will soon be for naught."

Elinor pursed her lips, then nodded. "All right. Then I will help you."

"And so will I," Abigail said.

"How hard can it be?" Guinevere muttered.

The door had been splintered at its center as well as near its lock. Because of the central buckling, it hung awkwardly on the hinge and the handle no longer lined up the doorjamb.

"I think that if we straighten this out, perhaps by nailing another board across it, we won't even need to remove it from the hinges," Guinevere said. Seemed easy and logical from how she looked at it.

"But how will you hammer it?" Abigail asked.

"Go and stand behind it," Guinevere said, picking up a board. "Hold it steady while I nail it in. Easy." However, the piece proved too long. "Only a minor setback." She worried her lip, trying to think like a carpenter. "We need a saw. Elinor, will you go and fetch one?"

Her maid nodded solemnly, avoiding eye contact, a telling sign she was about to do exactly the opposite.

Guinevere wagged a finger at her friend, giving her a fierce glower. "Don't even think about questioning the Marischal about this door business."

Elinor's shoulders sagged and she rolled her eyes. "Aye, my lady."

With Elinor slinking away, Guinevere sipped at the small ale a servant had brought up with her morning meal. It was lukewarm and not particularly tasty. She longed for the days at home in England. Mother would have a delicious elderflower wine set out and, instead of hammering away at a stubborn door, she'd be relaxing and perhaps writing a bit of poetry. Or creating a new pattern she could sew.

"Do you think the Marischal will require you to help in the rebuild of the kirk, too?" Abigail asked, her face screwed up with worry. "I'm not certain I'd be much help. A door is one thing, but a building? And one in which we worship. If I messed that up, would God ever forgive me?"

"I do not think he would," Guinevere murmured, glancing out the window where the men were still busy clearing away rubble from the fire and battle. "But, to be honest, I have no inkling as to what goes through that man's mind. If you'd asked me yesterday if I'd be fixing a door, I might have laughed in your face."

Elinor returned a short time later and brought with her the stable lad who she'd gotten the saw from.

"My lady." The lad rushed forward, worry creasing his brow. His clothes were clean pressed, smelling only slightly of manure and though his nails were permanently stained underneath, his hands looked mostly clean. "I ken ye dinna want any help in repairing the door, but if I could saw the wood for ye, I'd be most honored."

Guinevere studied the lad who couldn't have been more than fifteen. He looked worried, as though if she denied him, he'd be in quite a lot of trouble. Another test?

"All right. You may saw the wood." She gave him the measurement she needed and he quickly went to work on a wooden beam, brandishing her with just the right length. "Lovely, thank you. Now, Abigail, go and stand behind the door."

"If I may, my lady?" the lad said.

"All right, if you must," Guinevere said, taking note of Abigail's sigh of relief.

The lad held the door steady, while Elinor and Abigail held the wooden beam across it. Each of them tried to hide their fear when Guinevere started to hammer, the ladies yelping with each pound of the nail into the wood, and the stable lad holding his breath until his face turned purple.

But it wasn't working. The beam just slid, hanging awkwardly from the door and then falling off, nearly catching her toes in the process.

Guinevere let out a frustrated growl, hands slapping against her thighs.

"May I offer a suggestion?" The lad held up his hands in surrender and backed away as though he expected her to beat him for speaking. Just what rumors had gone on about her. "Only because I've had to fix a few stable doors from horses kicking at them."

"You may." Guinevere could use all the help she could get. Not only had she never fixed a door, she'd not seen one fixed either. She was working completely blind and, so far, every idea she'd had failed miserably.

"I think it would be easier if we took the door off the hinges, laid it upon the floor and pushed the splintered pieces back together. Or we could replace the splintered pieces all together, my lady."

"Hmm." Guinevere pretended to think about it. "Aye, a good idea, indeed. Let's replace them. I would be lost without your help."

The lad's face turned bright red at her compliment, and while he did offer her direction for the remainder of the project, she insisted on doing the job herself. Several hours later, when the door was hung back on the hinges, she beamed at their work. Unless someone knew exactly how the door looked before, or they took note of the dull gray old wood against the newer, fresher wood, they'd never know it was a brand new door. 'Twas beautiful.

"Thank you so very much," she said. "I just realized, I don't know your name."

"Henry, my lady."

"Why don't you go to the kitchens and tell Mrs. Donald I said you could have something sweet to eat."

Henry's face paled and he shook his head emphatically. "I daren't, my lady. 'Twas pleasure enough to help ye."

"Oh," Guinevere mused, trying to think of some other prize.

But all the while, he was backing up, muttering, "If ye'll excuse me, my lady, I must be returning to my duties afore I'm missed."

"Well, that was odd," Elinor said, staring through the empty door where the lad had been a moment ago.

"Very," Guinevere agreed. Why was he so against getting a treat for his hard work. She'd have to get something from the kitchens herself and take it to him as a thank you.

"I'm exhausted," Abigail said.

"Aye. Let's see how Claudia is doing and have a servant bring up the noon meal."

Hours later, when the late afternoon sun beamed through the coolness of her chamber, Guinevere smiled at her ladies. They'd managed to clean up her chamber, righting the wardrobe with the help of Henry—all too happy to return and be of use—and one of his friends.

Mrs. Donald, who asked to be called simply Cook, seemed miffed with Guinevere when she'd appeared with the nooning—a meal Guinevere could do without in the future—

of leftover porridge with a few gristly pieces of meat and root vegetables mixed in. Cook had called it leftover gruel and swore that everyone was eating it, but a glance out the window showed the men working on the outbuildings were eating hunks of roasted meat and fresh baked bread, while it appeared she and her ladies had been regulated to pig feed.

Cook informed her that the Marischal would be eating with his men and they'd not make use of the great hall unless an important guest arrived. That Guinevere and her ladies were to take their meals in her chamber. So separated from him. They'd had that one intimate moment the night before where she sobbed all over his shirt and now she was regulated to practically a prisoner in her rooms.

Well, that suited her just fine. Though she had hopes that supper would prove more appetizing. She'd rather not interact with her husband or his men, however, she suspected, at some point, being stuck behind the walls of her chamber for endless days would start to drive her mad. Well, maybe, but that moment they'd shared, it had changed something between the two of them. It had been so intimate. So eye opening. It was terrifying, actually. She'd never allowed a man to get that close to her and never had a man open up to her the way he had, even if she could tell he held a piece of himself back.

The remainder of the day, she paced her room, only taking time from that task to relieve herself and to look out the small window to see if Brody was still working with his men. Which he was nearly every time. Wasn't he going to come and see her progress on the door?

Alas, she was mistaken—he did not come to see the door and her supper was just as foul. They were served the same meal that evening that they'd been served that morning, with wine that tasted sour as though it had sat in the sun spoiling. Guinevere tossed her cup out the window, wincing when it landed on one of the Scots below.

"Apologies!" she called down. "Saints, but that will likely get me in trouble with the Marischal."

Elinor made a disapproving noise. "And what, will he finally make his face known to you? Come to see your progress on the door?"

Guinevere frowned at her lady and went to stare out the window at the bustle in the bailey. The sun had set, but the men still worked by the light of the torches. Hundreds of them, all intent on getting their tasks done before they collapsed for the night. It reminded her of an ant hill, where every little roving body had a job to do.

She'd not seen Brody at all since that afternoon.. He had his leine sleeves rolled up, exposing the tanned, slick, muscled skin of his forearms. His hair had been pulled back, but pieces had fallen against his face and he kept shaking his head to rid him of the tickling bits. She'd watched him pull a wagon, hoist stone, and nail boards. It appeared that the man she married was more than simply a lord, a marshal, and warrior.

This man was working right alongside his men and she saw more men from the villages than she'd ever seen before. Though, she wasn't surprised at the latter.

When the baron had landed here over a year before, she and her ladies had remained aboard the ship. Even from the decks of the mighty *Mary*, she could see the people fleeing from the castle, the woven fabrics of their plaids flying in the wind they created with their speed.

121

And she'd felt bad for them then. Knew they must be frightened for their lives. Had vowed at that moment, that whatever servants the baron could manage to keep, that she would be kind to them. Treat them as if they were one and the same as those who served her parents. One with her.

No better. No worse.

And she'd done that. Even helped in the gardens and kitchen. Delivered food and herbal tinctures to the poor. Summoned the healer if needed. Tended children and told stories beneath a shaded tree in the summer. Made them blankets to keep warm.

Guinevere had tried.

And she would continue to try, no matter what. Why not?

Even her ladies, stout Elinor, timid Abigail and worrisome Claudia had started to warm to the people.

Until Brody and Wallace had seized the castle, murdering all the English except for the four of them.

Guinevere's blood ran cold.

What if the baron had insisted she go with him? What if he'd forced her into that church? She'd not be alive right now.

She supposed she should be thankful that his cowardice had made him just as careless in regards to her as it had the entire year they were married. He'd not summoned her, shouted for her. Nothing. When the siege had begun, it had been she who'd barred the door. She who'd forced her ladies to help in pushing the wardrobe.

Likewise, none of the servants had tried to help her, no matter how much she had tried to get along with them.

Suddenly, she wasn't feeling so well. Her head hurt, throat was dry, and stomach was rolling. An uncontrollable anger flooded her blood. She wanted to hit someone. To hurt someone. To draw blood. And the only person she could think of was Brody Keith, her husband. This was his fault.

"I am tired," she said to no one in particular. "I think I should like to lie down."

Guinevere stood up from the small, round table where she'd been picking at her leftover gruel and moved toward her bed.

She sank down onto its softness, closing her eyes and tucking her fingers beneath her cheeks.

"Shall we undress you, my lady?" Elinor asked.

"Nay, nay," Guinevere said. "I shall undress myself later. Why do you not retire to your chamber and I shall see you in the morning."

Her ladies started to protest, but she mentioned a megrim, and they knew in short that the only thing to help that would be to leave her alone.

And so she was, in the quiet of her room, staring up at the woven canopy above her head, a bed that she'd never made love in, a virgin, married for the second time.

"Lord help me," she whispered. "For I want to sin."

CHAPTER ELEVEN

Darkness reached for him, but some invisible force held back any slumber that should come to Brody. After three sleepless nights, he should have fallen quickly, but instead his eyes refused to shut.

He lay on a chaise in the master's study—his study. A place where countless other heads had no doubt lain after late nights reading over missives, plotting, praying. Silver slices of the moon stabbed through the window, cutting across the trestle table where maps of his new holding were laid out, various pieces of wood carvings or stones to show villages, mills, and the like.

The surrounding villagers had arrived yesterday, paying him homage, bringing gifts which helped to refill some of their stores, and in return, he listened to their grievances and offered solutions—which were thankfully not disquieting. He was surprised to find that after a year of English rule, the people still had spirit.

The people were thrilled to have Dunnottar back in the hands of the Scots, though many grumbled at his choice in wife, there were just as many who whispered her praises. It seemed in the short time Guinevere had been here, she had made an impression on many with her kindness and good works. There was so much more to her than he realized. So much more to her than he would have ever given an Englishwoman credit for, and yet, he could have guessed. She was haughty and stubborn with him, but there was kindness, too. She'd stood up to him to protect her women, instead of cowering behind them, tossing them to the wolves.

Though he hated to admit it, she'd affected him in some way, made him feel soft toward her.

For that very reason, he'd spent the last few days avoiding her. Likewise, she seemed to be avoiding him as he'd not seen her once in the great hall for the evening meal, nor in the morning when the chaplain gave mass and then they broke their fast. At first, he'd thought she was trying to prove a point, but then Mrs. Donald told him that his wife had requested peace and solitude for prayer and reflection.

That was something he had to respect whether he wanted to or not.

Brody flopped his arm across his face and adjusted his body on the chaise. Visions of Guinevere's porcelain face, golden hair, bright blue-green eyes and cherry lips kept floating behind his closed lids, so he popped them open. Still, the images didn't fade.

125

There were two thoughts that continued to cross his mind. One—how desperately he wanted to kiss his wife, and two—that it would be best if he left in the morning for Ettrick Forest if he was to honor her wishes of three months.

Perhaps when the sun rose, he could accomplish both of those things. A kiss for the road. A fare-thee-well.

Perhaps she'd be pleased to see him go. Och, who was he kidding? She'd probably be thrilled to be rid of him for months on end.

Noah was desperate to join Wallace. They'd gotten news late in the evening that all was ready at Ettrick and the men would be marching toward the border in a few days' time. There was still a slight chance they could meet up with them, if they rode hard.

Having made the decision to leave, Brody's mind seemed to be put at ease and he fell into a dreamless sleep, waking with the rising of the sun. Brody washed up, gave orders to the seneschal to stand in his stead for any major needs of the castle. He'd brought his own seneschal, Artair, from his castle in East Lothian, promoting another in Artair's stead. Together, Artair and Mrs. Donald would be able to set the castle to rights. Guinevere could help them, as she had been here longer than the three of them, and by the time he returned from the siege in England, the castle defenses should be shored up, the outbuildings and kirk rebuilt, and Dunnottar once more restored to its is formidable glory.

And his wife... She should be ready to receive him properly.

Brody trudged through the great hall, headed toward the stairs. Though he'd avoided her for the better part of the last few days, it wouldn't do to simply leave for months on end—

especially if something were to happen to him in battle—without at least informing her of his departure.

Climbing the stairs, he came upon Mrs. Donald. She carried a tray of food that smelled most foul.

"Goodness, what is that?" Brody wrinkled his nose.

"Och! My laird!" Mrs. Donald seemed genuinely startled to see him, jerking to the side, her shoulder hitting the wall and the entire tray falling to the stairs. "Ye scared me." Her voice was accusing as they both stared down at the spilled food.

If it could even be called that.

A rotten looking porridge slipped from the broken pots in a puddle of something that very much resembled vomit.

"Ye were nay going to serve that to someone were ye?" Lord, but he wanted to get away from it. He had to grind his teeth to keep his lip from quivering, a sure sign he was about to toss up his breakfast.

Mrs. Donald cleared her throat. "Aye. The ladies."

Brody's eyes widened and he put his hands to his hips. "The *ladies*? As in my wife, your mistress? There had better be a good explanation as to why ye are feeding my wife garbage."

"'Tis not garbage exactly, my laird, but leftover gruel. In her moments of repentance she requested to only be fed such. And for ye not to visit."

Brody frowned, ignoring the last part. "And what in bloody hell is leftover gruel and why is it being served to your mistress?"

Mrs. Donald bristled, but quickly hid her reaction in the face of something more subservient. Brody wasn't fooled by

127

her odd behavior. He'd known the woman for years and this was the oddest she'd ever behaved.

"Her ladyship and her maids requested to be fed such at every meal." Mrs. Donald shrugged. "A penance, I suppose."

"Penance?"

"Begging your pardon, my laird, but I dinna try to make sense of what I'm told, just make certain I do it."

Brody narrowed his eyes, still not completely believing the older woman. There was something suspicious in her stance, besides the fact that the meal smelled horrendous.

"Go back to the kitchen and bring my wife and her ladies the same meal ye planned to serve me this morn. Tell her I insisted. And never feed her anything less than what ye'd serve me."

Mrs. Donald's face flamed red and she started to sputter, but he held up his hand.

"Ye needn't fuss, Cook, simply explain that a lady of the house does not eat food fit only for a mutt." Brody didn't wait for the woman to make more of a protest. His wife shouldn't eat that shite, and if she took issue with that, simply being told it was his wish for her to eat good food should suffice.

In fact, perhaps he should mention that to her now.

Brody marched the rest of the way up the stairs, coming to halt outside of the freshly built door of her chamber.

"Ballocks," he muttered. He'd completely forgotten about the door. Even though she'd told him she didn't want him to fix it, he'd planned on it. Only he'd gotten so distracted with his other duties, he'd completely slacked.

Well, at least someone had gotten around to shoring up where he'd slackened.

Brody raised his hand to knock when one of her ladies appeared as though from nowhere in the corridor, melting from the shadows as if she'd been waiting for him. Elinor, he was pretty certain, the tough one.

"Marischal," she said, her eyes narrowed to slits.

"My lady." He bowed slightly.

"Might I have a word?" She brushed her hand through the air, pointing toward the door. "My lady is indisposed at the moment."

"Aye." Brody backed away from the door, arms crossed. He leaned against the wall opposite his wife's room and waited for the lady's maid to declare whatever it was she had in mind. Perhaps more of what Mrs. Donald have spoken of—repentance, peace and reflection.

"May I have your permission to speak frankly?" she asked, her gaze not wavering, but strong, challenging.

Brody pursed his lips. Elinor reminded him a lot of Guinevere and, in that case, he wasn't certain he wanted to hear what she had to say. All the same, he inclined his head.

"My lady has worked most hard to please you over the past few days, but I must say I think..." She swallowed, seeming to lose some of her courage.

"Please, go on," Brody said, trying to keep his voice calm. What had he missed? He wracked his brain. He'd not heard hide nor hair of her for several days.

Elinor squared her shoulders, pressed her lips together, shifting once and then blurting out, "You have been treating her like a prisoner. Making demands of her that are not fit for a lady."

"What?" Brody started, pushing off from the wall, only realizing at the last second how his body language came off as aggressive and so he settled back again. "How so?"

The door yanked opened and, there, standing in the center was his beautiful wife glowering at the both of them. Saints, but he'd noticed her beauty before, but with the light of the morning sun shining golden around her luscious locks, she looked like an angel. An angel bent on telling them both her mind.

"My lady," he said, bowing before her. Brody took her hand and brought it to his lips, breathing in the floral scent of her skin. "Ye look lovely this morning."

"Thank you," she murmured, smoothing her skirts. Her gaze roved over him, and she said. "You look rather menacing, in a good, overlord sort of way."

Brody chuckled. "May I come in?"

Beside him Elinor still stood stony. She interrupted only to excuse herself and slipped past Guinevere, gathering the other two ladies and disappearing into the chamber they shared, leaving him alone with his wife.

"I'm surprised you ask," she said. "You've been most adamant about keeping me away."

Lord, but he had been avoiding her, but she had to know, he wasn't completely to blame.

"How have your days of peace and reflection gone?"

She looked at him as though he'd grown a second head. "You do have the oddest things to say."

"Let me guess, 'tis not appropriate to ask."

Guinevere backed up a step, sweeping her arm wide and allowing him entry. "Do come in." Her voice had taken on a very serious and formal tone.

The room was much cleaner than when he'd last seen it, which had been when he'd banged down the door.

"I see the door is repaired," he said, giving another appreciative glance at how seamless the new boards melded with the old.

Guinevere beamed, folding her hands before her as though she'd built the thing herself. "Aye."

"Ye are pleased, then," he said.

"I am. Are you not?"

Brody nodded. "I will give my thanks to whomever it is that built it for ye."

She cocked her head. "Certainly you jest."

Och, but the lady was a conundrum. "Why would I not show gratitude?"

"But..." She wrinkled her pert nose. "I built it, as *ye* requested."

"As I...?" Brody trailed off, then burst into laughter. "Ye jest! A good one, my lady."

His wife did not laugh. In fact, she looked offended. As if he'd just told her she smelled like a dung heap. "A good one? I do not jest." The seriousness in her tone and the way she stood on edge, ready to slug him, did not seem humorous at all.

What in blazes... "Ye built this?" Brody took a step back to admire the craftsmanship. He stroked a hand over the boards.

"Aye. With the help of my ladies and a stable lad."

"Ah." Brody understood now. The stable lad must have done the work while she oversaw it. "A job well done then."

"You don't believe me. Well, no matter. I know each nail I hammered through the wood, and have the splinters and a bruised thumb to prove it." She held up her hands, evidence that, indeed, she had put them to work.

Brody reached for her hands, sliding his fingers over her palms and fingertips. There were callouses where each finger met her palm, her thumb was bruised beneath the knuckle, and several spots that looked to be deeply rooted splinters, reddened around the pieces of wood, the beginnings of an infection. It appeared that she had, indeed, taken part in building the door, and had the battle wounds to prove it.

"I'm impressed. Apologies for doubting ye."

"Thank you." Pride beamed in her stance.

"Did ye not try to get these out?" he asked softly, taking a look at her splinters. "They're starting to get infected and will become so if we dinna remove them."

"I tried, but they are so deep." She frowned up at him. "I thought perhaps they would come out on their own."

"Have ye never gotten a splinter before? Even as a wee lass?"

Guinevere shook her head. "Not that I can remember. My days were spent studying mostly and learning the duties I would perform as mistress of my own castle. The only thing not related to being a lady was when my father taught us how to use a dagger to defend ourselves."

The ways of the English were not so different from the Scots, save for his parents had done a better service to his sisters, teaching them a little bit of labor work, too. He was impressed her father had taught her to defend herself. That was a skill not all ladies possessed.

"I see. We mustn't leave the bits of wood to fester beneath the skin. Will ye let me try to get them out?"

She looked skeptical. "Would it not be better to see the healer? I don't want to burden you."

"'Tis no burden. Now be still a moment. This may sting."

Brody went to work first on the splinter on the edge of her hand between her thumb and forefinger. He pinched the skin to see the insertion point and she gasped.

"Ouch."

"I'm sorry, lass. Shall I give ye a wee nip of whisky to take the edge off?"

She shook her head, closed her eyes. "I'd rather just be done with it. Do your worst."

Brody chuckled. "The worst of the pain will soon be over. It hurts because the splinter is buried deep and because it is getting infected. Once it's out, ye'll be right as rain."

"I'm ready."

He squeezed again, pressing his thumbnail at the base of the splinter and easing it out through the opening in her skin.

The second splinter along her finger was not as accommodating. The bugger wouldn't budge and a tear had formed at the corner of her eye.

"I'm sorry for hurting ye, lass. Have ye a pitcher of water?" he asked.

"Aye." She opened her eyes and moved to the basin, discreetly swiping at the tear. By the time she returned to him, she looked ready to do battle once more.

"We need to soak your hand a minute to loosen it." Brody poured the water for her and gently placed her hand into the basin, stroking his fingers over the back of her hand.

"Have you removed many splinters?" she asked, wiggling her fingers in the water. "You seem to be an expert."

Brody chuckled softly and nodded. "Aye. From myself. My sisters. My men."

"Ye've sisters?" Her eyes brightened.

Brody's smile fell, his chest constricting. For a brief moment with her, he'd forgotten his pain. "One."

"But ye said—"

He cut her off, not wanting to share. "One. Maire." He lifted her hand to examine the splinters. The edges of the skin around the wound looked looser.

Guinevere studied him with roving, inquisitive eyes and he tried to ignore her, but it was hard. She didn't believe him. And he wasn't surprised.

He put her hand back into the water and mumbled, "Just a moment longer."

"I've three sisters," she murmured, returning her attention to the basin. "They are all at home, unmarried. Where is your sister, Maire?"

Brody cleared his throat. "Home with my mother."

"She is younger?"

"Aye."

"Have you any brothers?"

"None."

"Me either." She beamed up at him. "Something we have in common then. We are both the oldest, with no brothers."

Brody nodded, not wanting to keep talking about his family. The heavy black cloud of his failure, his inability to protect, the one thing he'd been trained for his entire life, loomed near. Made it doubly important he keep his wife safe. And yet… He'd come up here to tell her he was leaving.

"Does your family live near Dunnottar?" she asked.

"Two days' ride, if I'm quick. Three or four if weather slows me down."

"Do you think…" She chewed her lip. A plump pink one that made his thoughts of kissing return. "Do you think I'll get a chance to meet them?"

"Nay." He said it too quickly, even he realized that.

Sadness filled here eyes. "I suppose you'll never meet my family either."

"A pity if your sisters are as beautiful as ye are."

A pretty pink colored her skin. "They are much prettier."

"I doubt that."

"I suppose I'll never get to see them again either." The great sadness that colored her words clutched at his heart.

"Perhaps ye will. This war cannot last forever."

Distracted by his own admissions, he plucked her hand from the water and went to work on the second splinter. It easily came out, as did the third.

Brody swiped away the droplets of blood and brought her fingers to his lips, kissing them.

"All better, now," he said.

"Aye," she whispered. Her eyes met his and this time, Brody couldn't hold back.

He leaned forward and brushed his mouth over hers. A gentle, soft kiss, but one in which he poured out his soul.

There was something about Guinevere. Something that drew him in. Opened him up. And he didn't like that. Didn't like that she could cause him to forget himself.

What was the harm in kissing her though? She was his wife after all. And he should consider himself lucky that he was attracted to her. Shouldn't he?

Besides he was leaving soon…

135

Guinevere didn't pull away from him. Didn't try to remind him that he'd promised not to bed her. She leaned into him. Her tiny hands clutched at his shirt near his shoulders.

And she sighed, proof of her letting go to some part of the wall that she, too, had built up around her.

Chapter Twelve

Heat surrounded Guinevere.

A budding feeling inside her limbs that she could only guess was desire, stirred. The way he'd expertly removed her splinters, so gentle, so filled with sweet softness.

Guinevere had never desired a man before, so this feeling, the sensations whipping through her, the ripples of pleasure… She knew them for what they were now. Brody had brought out these same feelings when he kissed her in the cave. The same tickle of need when he'd kissed her hand.

The insides of her cheek were so torn up from all the biting she'd been doing. The attempts to stop these feelings from happening.

But what could one kiss hurt? She'd not be taking him to bed. In fact, soon enough, she'd be able to plan her escape.

Until that time… A kiss. A simple kiss.

Seemed harmless enough.

Right?

Aye…

Guinevere slid her hands over his strong shoulders. Allowing herself a moment to simply escape from the realities of life and melt into this man's embrace. He smelled of leather, wool, and pine. A subtle measure of spice on his tongue as it swept over hers.

Brody's kiss was so different than anything she'd ever experienced before him. No naïve clashing of teeth and slobbering of tongue like the stable lad back in England when she'd been a girl. Or the boorish slathering her husband had attempted. Nor the dry brush of a family member's greeting.

This was sensual. Meant to elicit the stirrings of desire. Passion. Need. And it was working. Every part of her tingled with excitement. She melted against him.

Beneath her fingertips and the linen of his shirt, corded muscle rippled. Brody tugged her tighter to his body. Her breasts pushed against his chest, their hearts pounding on one another. His breath fanning over her face. His hands sliding up and down her spine. Thick thighs pressed to hers. Hips to hips. Toes to toes.

Guinevere could have let him kiss her all day and that was when she realized that giving in just a little bit was too much. Kissing him all day would only lead to other things—very specifically, the one thing she was trying to avoid. She didn't know why she held on to her virginity like it was gold, except that in this day and age, it was the only thing she could use as a bartering chip for a better marriage.

But she was already married.

Twice now.

Oh, saints! But was this her mind's way of trying to convince her to let go? Nay! This was why she couldn't kiss him all day.

With her hands pressed to his shoulders, she gave him a gentle push, releasing her mouth from his and sucking in a deep, much needed breath.

"I seem to have... gotten away with myself," she muttered, feeling the need to make an excuse for kissing him in return.

"There is nothing wrong with kissing, Guinevere." Brody slid a finger along the curve of her cheek. "We *are* married."

"Aye." She flicked her gaze back up toward his, taking him in, really seeing him.

He was handsome. Skin darkened from the sun, hair the color of night, and eyes that she could have stared at all day. Oh, goodness… Staring at him, kissing him, all through the day. What had gotten into her? *He* had. The man had bewitched her. His chivalry, his torment, his kiss. 'Twas a potent draught, intoxicating her.

But more so than simply on a physical level. Ever since meeting him, she'd sensed the haunting in his eyes, the wounded look he tried to hide. And the charitable part of herself that needed to help others reached out, clutching to that.

Brody had mentioned sisters. She'd been certain of the plural connotation and yet when she'd asked, he'd insisted he had only one.

What happened to his other sister or sisters? Had they passed away? Run away? Otherwise been separated? Curiosity flooded her. She wanted to know, but etiquette bade her not mention it beyond what she had. At least not yet.

Perhaps in time he'd feel free to share it with her. The demons that rocked him, they would forever keep a wedge between himself and anyone else.

Oh, she could probably wriggle the information out of his cousin, Noah. However, she hated to go behind his back, and why she should care, she didn't have the answer to that, either.

Lord, help her, he was getting inside her head. Making her care about things she had no business caring over.

They needed distance. Why was it every time they were together, they seemed to share these deep moments?

He needed to leave the chamber. She needed him to stop looking at her with those dark, intense eyes. Needed a moment to catch her breath, something to divert her from all the bewildering thoughts going through her head.

"I should let you get back to your duties." Guinevere turned away from him, shuffling toward the window and hoping that was enough of a subtle hint for him to leave her be.

"My lady…" Brody's voice was hoarse, choked sounding.

She turned back around, leaning a hip on the windowsill and catching the struggle on his face that he tried to hide. Emotion welled in her chest. Why did he have to look at her like that? Why did his expression mirror her own thoughts?

Brody ran his hand through his dark hair. "I want ye to be happy here."

"Happy?" Why? *Why* did he have to care? "Will you be?"

He cocked his head at her, seeming surprised at her question, as though he'd not thought of himself, but she knew that wasn't true. Not since he'd shared with her a few days ago how he felt about being married.

"A warrior does not often consider his happiness, but rather his duty." That sounded more like him. The warrior side. The side that hid the heart he had.

Well, if he wanted to play it out that way, then she would, too. "And a lady does the same," she quipped back.

Brody pursed his lips, crossed his arms over his chest, a subtle clue that she was no longer allowed to see inside him. She mirrored his movements without realizing it and then shoved her hands down to her sides.

"Aye. We both have our duties." The way he nodded his head so curtly, made it seem like his words were meant more for himself than for her. He sucked in a deep breath, prepared to say more.

"Aye," she cut him off before he could begin. She didn't want to hear it. "You spend an awful lot of time trying to see to my happiness. Trying to please me. 'Tis not the way it is done."

Brody groaned. "I do. And I dinna plan to change it, even if ye are resistant to it." Brody scrubbed a hand over his face. "Believe it or not, I may have sieged this castle, inadvertently causing the death of your husband, and now ye find yourself wed to me. A warrior, a leader, would tell ye this is the price we all pay for war. That it is to be expected. That ye should accept it. But the honorable side of me, that part says I must apologize. That I must treat ye kindly. And I plan to do so, even if ye push me back. And I hope in time, ye'll respect me for it."

Guinevere's chest constricted. "You're a very different sort of man, Brody Keith."

"What do ye mean by that?" His brow furrowed.

Guinevere swallowed. "Part warrior, part man with a heart."

His chest puffed as though she'd offended him. "Make no mistake, I am all warrior."

"They are all the pieces of you," she whispered, lowering her gaze to the floor. Why was it so hard to breathe? "I suppose I should consider myself lucky." Guinevere licked her lower lip, raising her eyes to consider the man standing before her. He'd opened himself up to her, even if he didn't realize it. Perhaps, she could make a confession to him, though not her deepest secret, she could feel him out for his reaction. "I'll be honest with you, Brody." Her fingers folded into her robe and she tucked it tighter around her. "Perhaps my ways are not always right. I was not happily married before."

"Nay?" Though he questioned her, he didn't sound at all surprised.

"Not at all." She looked out at the landscape, the bustling bodies, the swaying trees in the distance. The scent of peat fires rose up in the air, imbuing the air with their heady aroma. "Our marriage was arranged. De Ros was promised my father's land and title upon his passing. The ships of his fleet were part of my dowry. I'd not be surprised if the baron hadn't been planning my father's death on the side. You might have burned down a holy building, but he murdered many of the men of God who lived here before. He was a cruel man. A selfish man. There was no love between us. And I know it is a sin for me to speak of him this way, as we should never speak ill of the dead, but it is the truth. So when you say you want me to be happy, I mean what I say that you are a different sort of man. Most do not consider a woman's happiness, not even her acceptance or agreement. I am honor bound and duty bound to remain by your side, to treat you as you should be treated, to never stray. But..." Guinevere shivered, hoping she'd not gone too far with her confession. "I cannot promise my happiness, as it has never been an assured thing."

"I thank ye for sharing that with me, my lady." Brody stepped forward, then paused. "I know ye've no cause to believe me, but ye can trust me, Guinevere. That man, de Ros, he is gone, and I am nothing like him. I will keep ye safe. I will keep ye well. I will honor ye."

"I do believe you will try," she said. "I've not known you long, my laird, but from what I have seen, you mean to honor your word."

"Then why do I hear doubt in your voice?"

Guinevere smiled sadly. "We can all make promises, but we cannot all keep them. Only time will tell."

"I gave ye my blood oath. Only death can hold me back from keeping my promises to ye."

"Then I pray you live a long and healthy life." She let out a short, quiet laugh. "For I'd hate to be married a third time."

Brody grinned, showing his strong, healthy teeth. "I shall endeavor to remain alive. Which brings me to the reason I came to see ye this morning."

Guinevere bit the inside of her cheek to keep from asking why it had taken him three days to see her to begin with, then winced at the bruising she'd created from biting so many times.

The brightness of the morning sun was suddenly clouded over, leaving shadows to bounce around the room. Brody watched his wife, the way she hesitated, as though the floor were made of broken glass and the air of iron nails. She moved so gracefully, gently, cautiously. Fingers sliding over her arms, hip slowly popping out to one side as she shifted her weight from one foot to the other. Even the small dimple in her cheek he could tell was from her biting it. As much as he wanted to put off what needed to be said, there was no getting around it.

With a deep breath, he blurted out, "I came to say goodbye."

"Goodbye?" She frowned, those slim fingers which had curled around his shirt, now curled around her own sleeves. "Where are you going?"

"I must rejoin my men at the border. We are at war."

"The border. War." She rolled the words on her tongue, and very obviously found them distasteful.

"Aye. There is still much to be done. Our fight against the English is still young."

Guinevere looked him dead in the eye, the look of betrayal there almost hidden but not quite. He'd just gotten done telling her that he'd give her his blood oath and now he was leaving, giving her no choice but to distrust his word. Damnation!

Why did she look so disappointed? Wasn't this what she wanted? More distance? The way she kept backing up made it seem so and yet...

"And who is to keep the castle safe?"

He knew what she really meant. Who was to keep *her* safe if he was leaving? "My seneschal, Artair, from Keith Marischal has arrived. He will make certain that the holding, castle and repairs run smoothly. You'll have Mrs. Donald to help with the care of the keep, and I will leave my trusted guard and cousin, Anderson, in charge of security."

"Oh." Guinevere chewed her lip, absorbing what he'd said. And then her gaze flitted from his to the floor, her shoulders slumping. "How long will you be gone?"

He'd not expected her to be disappointed. He'd not expected to see such dejection in her stance. Zounds, but it made him want to reach out to her. To tug her into his arms. But he knew the time for holding her had passed and there was little he could do about it now. "I dinna know. Perhaps a few months at least, a year at most."

Guinevere nodded slowly, but before she could respond there was a knock at the door. Mrs. Donald entered quietly, not meeting either of their gazes as she delivered a tray to Guinevere's table. As soon as the dishes were set down, the cook rushed from the room.

He spotted his wife eyeing the plate of boiled eggs, pork and biscuits with jam.

"A true breakfast," she murmured, her eyes lighting up and giving away how famished she must have been.

If he'd only been served slop for days, he'd have starved!

"I'm afraid I caused a mishap with your morning meal on the stairs. I bade Mrs. Donald to bring ye another, and I daresay the fare should be much better than the first I beheld."

"Oh…" She turned away from him.

"I dinna mean to displease ye," Brody said. "But there are certain things a lady should eat and certain things she should not."

Guinevere whipped around at that, eyes narrowed to slits, and her hands fisted at her sides. "Your message is perfectly clear, Marischal."

"Ye dinna agree?" he asked, confused. "Do ye not like eggs?"

"Does it matter? Ye've made it clear ye dinna see me as your equal."

"My equal? But we are not the same." What man and woman were?

"And don't I know it?"

"As do I," he drawled out, feeling as though he were missing something. What was happening right now? Why did he feel that they were arguing about something completely different from each other? "Ye're a woman, an English woman at that. A lady, born and raised. I am warrior, Scottish to the bone. We could not be more worlds apart than that, and yet here we are, bound to one another for eternity."

Guinevere bristled, as though he'd reminded her of something she found quite foul.

"Well"—she waved her hand toward the door, dismissing him—"best be on your way. There are more English to maim and murder after all."

Lord, but this was not going the way he thought at all. He'd wanted to kiss her. He'd wanted her to get that bemused look on her face as she had the very first time he'd kissed her.

He wanted her to miss him.

An odd thought given she barely knew him. And yet, it seemed a comfort that when he'd go to battle, his wife would be thinking of him back home.

Home. That was what Dunnottar was now.

"All right." He hated the small hint of dejection in his tone. "I shall return."

"Or not," she murmured, crossing her arms over her chest.

Ouch. That stung worse than a blade to the gut. Brody nodded and turned to leave. She marched behind him, shutting the door at his back, before he could say anything else.

Brody touched the wood of the door, wanting to start over again. If he could, he'd march in once more, announce that he'd ordered her a breakfast fit for a queen, and that he wished for a kiss to keep him sane the cold nights he'd be spending at camp. He'd remove her splinters, kissing each wound and then tell her to be safe, that he'd miss her while away.

Alas, she shut the door in his face.

Brody trudged toward the stairs, shaking his head and wondering if he'd ever be able to make things right with her. And then doubting if it was even worth it. Perhaps, they'd been doomed from the start. He had no right to take someone else under his wing when he'd so utterly failed in caring for his own to begin with. Their torment and deaths would forever lay over him. How could he even ask for any happiness on earth when his sister could never smile again?

Chapter Thirteen

"How long has it been?" Elinor sat down beside Guinevere at the trestle table where she'd been sorting dried herbs and flowers to be mixed with the rushes.

Pretending nonchalance, Guinevere shrugged, "Since when?"

Elinor picked up a sprig of rosemary to smell it, raising a brow. "I've known you practically my whole life. I can tell when you're off. And you're definitely off, so no use in denying it. So, how long has it been?"

Guinevere plucked the rosemary sprig back from her friend and ran her nails down the side of the stem, removing the needles and adding them to her mixture. The question of how long it had been could be answered in any number of ways. How long had it been since they'd left England? How long had it been since she'd witnessed the baron murder monks and clergymen? How long had it been since she'd last let de Ros "lie" with her? How long had it been since Brody had set her free, only to grasp her for himself? And how long had it been since he'd kissed her? Or since he'd left?

Depending on how she answered, her clever lady's maid and friend would be able to garner just what had her moping these past few weeks since Brody had ridden off with his cousin, Noah, to conquer her countrymen.

The days were growing colder. And even if the Scots somehow miraculously won their battles, would he be able to travel in the dead of winter back to Dunnottar, or would he be stuck in England, giving his enemies a chance at revenge? The past winter had been brutal, and there had been several men from her husband's regiment who died of cold or lost limbs due to frostbite. Many of her own nights, she'd spent laying awake shivering in the dark. 'Twas one of the reasons she'd been so adamant about making blankets for the children of Dunnottar. If grown men were freezing, wouldn't they be?

So while her forethought was that she'd have to wait until spring to escape, else she get stuck, the question and worry that niggled the back of her mind now was, she prayed Brody made it safely back, if he made it off the battlefield with breath left in his body. Because she didn't want him to die.

Why did she worry over him? Och, but that was a question she refused to answer. Leave it simply to compassion.

They'd left each other on a bad note. But she still saw his image riding through the tunneled gates. The way he'd stopped on the hilltop beyond and turned around. She'd been watching. He'd raised his hand, and she'd raised hers in turn, hoping he saw her. Praying the raised hand was to her and not someone below.

When she'd looked down there had been no one there, leaving her to believe he had been, indeed, waving goodbye to her.

A truce?

Perhaps.

A safe answer to Elinor would be just how long they'd been in Scotland. "One year and two months, now." Guinevere pulled out another bunch of dried rosemary, removing the scented needles from their stem.

"When did you last have a letter from your family?" Elinor picked up another sprig of rosemary, helping to clear it of needles.

"Some months." She sighed. "I sent word a week ago when I could finally put pen to paper. I told them about the kirk and the death of de Ros. Not about Marischal Keith."

Elinor raised her brows, nodded, but said nothing about her withdrawal of the truth. "They will write you soon."

Guinevere nodded. "Aye." She scooped up a handful of dried heather, crumbling them into the rosemary needles.

What she really wanted to do was write a letter to Brody. But what could she say? That all was well at the castle? Wouldn't his seneschal write such?

The man he'd left in charge, Artair, was her father's age, but spry and vastly knowledgeable. He'd kept the repairs to the castle running smoothly and already a foundation had been laid for the new kirk. What was more, the man was nice to her, whereas Mrs. Donald appeared only to want to punish her. She still hadn't figured out exactly what the older woman was up to. Her animosity was real, that much was evident.

There had been no more slop for breakfast, of that Guinevere was grateful. Every meal was plentiful and delicious. But, she wondered how long the ruse would have been held up if Brody hadn't knocked it out of her hands? And how long it would last with him no longer at the castle demanding it be so.

Guinevere had come to realize that Cook had been playing them both on that chord. She never expected to get along with everyone, all the time. But on the same note, she'd really tried to be kind to everyone at the castle. Hopefully soon, Cook, would take notice.

And Brody...

She'd been harsh to him, said things that perhaps she shouldn't have before he left. The heat of the moment. She saw now that he'd only been kind to her. He'd not hit her, as most men would have for speaking to him with such cruel tones. In fact, the man had seemed positively perplexed when they argued. Which had convinced her that there was some sort of misunderstanding in regards to the topic of equality, food, the door. So perhaps, that was what she'd write him about. Ask him point blank. Clear things up. For if he did plan to return, and she'd not yet had a chance to escape, then maybe...

What?

This was where Guinevere often ran into conflict.

She'd been married to an Englishman. It had not been pleasant. Not that all Englishmen would be like de Ros, but how would she know? If she escaped, returned to England and her family, who was to say that she'd not be paired with another such man?

Brody, though he was Scottish and a barbarian, was kind to her. Vowed to keep her safe, even if he'd left her within a week of marriage. So far, he'd held true to that. He'd set her up with a good amount of security and able-bodied people. She was safe. Felt safe. He'd also kept his promise to not bed her just yet. As mad as it seemed, right now, Brody was the lesser of two evils.

And he wasn't even here.

She could go on living life here while he was away. Even if he returned, he'd likely go away again. He served the king. He could not always be at Dunnottar. It seemed infinitely better than being married off to someone else who could likely turn out like her first husband. Besides, however much she hated to admit it, she kind of liked Brody.

"Have you written your family about my releasing you?" Guinevere asked, changing the subject.

Another promise Brody had made good on, letting her ladies leave. Abigail and Claudia had ridden out with an escort the week before. She'd been sad to see them go, but the way they fainted at every footstep and shadow, she also felt a sense of relief.

They'd soon find their happiness, or at the very least, gain back some of the gumption they'd lost.

"I have." Elinor scooped up the crumbled mixture and put it in the bucket. "'Tis a shame we've no dried lemon or orange peels."

"Aye." Guinevere stopped what she was doing and touched the back of her friend's hand. "Have you heard back from your family? Have you decided when to rejoin them?"

A long sigh escaped her friend. "I am not leaving." Elinor finally met her gaze. "I told them this. I came to Scotland to serve as your lady's maid. I intend to continue my duties here, with you, for the foreseeable future."

Guinevere sat back, catching herself just as she leaned far enough to almost fall from the bench. A heavy weight settled on her shoulders. This was not the way it was supposed to be. Elinor was supposed to go home. Guinevere had saved her from a future in Scotland. "But, what of a marriage? Your happiness?"

Elinor laughed. "My happiness? Who says I am not happy now?"

Guinevere frowned. Elinor did seem quite content. "I admit that I do quite enjoy this to what fate awaits me in England."

"Aye. And think of what awaits me? Why not remain here with my dearest friend?"

Elinor was the youngest of twelve. Her father was a baron, and so she was a lady, but being the youngest, her prospects had been slim. It was marriage to a regimented man or serving with Guinevere. The convent had not been an option simply because two of her other sisters had taken their places in the church, and the dowers needed for such service were beyond the number allotted to Elinor—unless she went to a much poorer abbey which she'd not wanted, nor did her parents. She didn't have the disposition anyway. And marriage to a knight in the king's service, a man who would be happy with her small dowry? She'd threatened to slit her own throat, claiming that any such man to take such a small dower would only drink and gamble it away within a single night.

"I should have guessed." Guinevere smiled sadly. "I am pleased you'll be staying with me. I do enjoy your company."

"Me, too."

Guinevere hugged her friend and then whispered, "I don't think I'm going to try to escape."

Elinor nodded. "I didn't think so, either. So, now do you want to answer my question honestly?"

She pursed her lips. "What question?"

"How *long* has it *been*?"

Guinevere let out a soft chuckle. She knew exactly to what Elinor was referring—or to whom and when he'd left. "Three weeks and two days." Guinevere let out a long drawn out sigh. "I don't even like him. I barely know him. Why do I care about whether he lives or dies? Why have I counted the days since he left?"

Elinor shrugged. "Because. You're an honorable woman and you accepted him as your husband. 'Tis only natural to wonder about one's future. Besides, you're intrigued by the Marischal. He is different than de Ros. Besides being handsome, intelligent and witty, he is protective, chivalrous. All qualities that de Ros did not possess. 'Tis no wonder you're taken with him."

"He is different than any man I've ever met." Guinevere pulled at another stem of rosemary. "I am intrigued for certes." She nodded. "And aye, I think perhaps a little taken."

Elinor giggled. "He is very handsome."

"There is that. And tall. And strong. And..." She almost said that he was a good kisser, but that was not something ladylike to discuss, even if she did want to tell her friend how she'd melted in his arms. Elinor would know beyond any of her other friends, as she'd snuck with many a handsome knight to kiss under the moonlight. But that was a topic they'd never broached.

Elinor chewed her lip. "His cousin is also quite handsome."

"Noah?" Guinevere darted a glance at her. "I am sorry to say he is promised to another."

Elinor pouted. "A shame."

They finished working on the scented mixtures, then spread them through the great hall and their bed chambers. Now that Abigail and Claudia were gone, Elinor had a chamber to herself.

That evening, after a supper of fish in lemon sauce, when she was alone, Guinevere pulled out a piece of parchment, her ink and quill. The time had come for her to put her thoughts down, to send them off, and pray they were received well. She spread the paper out on the table, smoothing over the edges. A jumble of thoughts and ways in which to start tunneled through her mind. She waved them away and put the quill to the inkwell, then pressed it to the parchment.

My Dear Marischal Keith,

Nay. Dear was too... caring? But it was a formal greeting. Was it not? To late, she'd already written it in ink. If she scratched it out he would see that. Perhaps she should consider thinking more deeply about what to write... But her fingers continued to move.

I hope this letter finds you well.

Why did such a line sound so false? So uninteresting? She truly did wish him well, but it seemed unnatural to say such. Again, formal.

All is well here. We've already had a dusting of snow and even inside the castle, with a hearth blazing, and sitting beneath a blanket, I can see my breath in the air. How do men at camp keep warm at night? During the day? Are you in need of more blankets? Hose? I beg your forgiveness for my ignorance at what I should send. I've included a sachet of herbs and flowers for you to keep within your pillow. The lavender and chamomile scents will help you sleep at night, to keep your strength. Please let me know what else you or your men might require.

She was a terrible letter writer, she decided. And parchment was so expensive. Guinevere resisted the urge to toss it in the fire and, instead, sat back in her chair to contemplate what to write next. What did she truly want to say? Perhaps the best way to write it, was to simply write what came to mind—stop forcing out what she thought she was supposed to say. Enough with niceties. No beating around the bush. She wasn't the type to stall besides.

Guinevere was a lady of action.

Or at least, she wanted to be.

Taking a deep breath, she wrote the words she'd pondered for the better part of three weeks.

I admit my parting words were not as I would have liked them, given you were leaving for dangers unknown, and a time neither of us could guess at. I am sorry for wishing you ill, and I do, honestly, hope you are safe and unharmed. I am grateful to you for providing me protection and safety when you could have tossed me to the sea of unknown.

Though we find ourselves having stepped onto a path neither one of us wanted or could have envisioned, I do hope we can make the best of it. So as such, I must ask about the door. Was it a test? What did it mean? What do you expect from me?

Now, how should she sign it? Honorably? With regards? Guinevere settled, instead, for the truth, one she was trying to accept.

Your Wife,
Lady Keith

Guinevere reread the letter, and considered the flames in her hearth one more time, before finally folding it neatly around the small sachet she'd made and sealing it with wax. She'd no seal, nor a ring to mark the wax, and so she carved a *G* into it, hoping that would do.

The following morning, she gave the letter to one of Brody's men.

"Make certain you deliver this into his hands. And find out what news you can."

White clouds covered the sky. Snow would likely touch the ground before night fell. She could smell its scent in the air. Gentle waves of the sea lapped at the cliffs below, and all she could do was pray the messenger did not freeze before he made it to the border, before he found Wallace's camp and her husband.

She prayed Brody was still alive when he arrived.

He would have made it there by now. Wallace would have already begun an invasion. He could have already fought in a battle. That realization brought with it a whole host of unsightly visions. The clanking of swords, crushing blows, the way his weapon had dripped blood when he'd crashed through her door. And wounds... What if he was hurt? What if, while he fought one man, another jumped on his back? What if right now, he lay on the cold ground in a pool of his own blood? Or on a cot in a makeshift tent where inept men worked to seal his wounds and keep infection at bay?

Guinevere shuddered. *Pray, be well.*

When she turned around, Mrs. Donald was glowering at her from the top of the stairs outside of the keep. Her hands were on her hips. How long had the woman been watching her? Glaring at her? The woman was positively sour and it was no secret that she despised Guinevere. How could she convince the woman she was not the enemy? Perhaps that was a task she'd never be able to complete.

"Your breakfast is getting cold," Mrs. Donald barked. A stout dame of black and white. Scots against the English. Woman versus man. Noble versus common. There was no melding or in-between, but a line drawn in the sand. One had to choose which side they stood on.

"My thanks, Mrs. Donald." Guinevere gave the woman a cheerful smile that was not returned.

Mrs. Donald grunted and marched off with a huff.

One battle at a time, Guinevere supposed. One battle at a time.

Chapter Fourteen

"Ballocks." Brody was ankle deep in mud. "Better than shite," he said, with a raised brow at Noah.

They were trying to make the best of the siege on the border of England. A torrential downpour had pummeled their camp in Rothbury Forest. They'd been in Northumberland, England, for four days, soaked to the bone with rain that only abated at night to allow the chill wind to freeze the puddles into blocks of ice.

More than once Brody had woken with icicles in his hair.

After a long day, they'd finally returned, and while his horse was being looked after by his squire, Brody had sought a moment of privacy with his cousin to discuss the state of their men.

Their breaths left clouds of mist with every word.

"That is the truth." Brody rubbed at the stubble on the cold skin of his face. "How do the men fare? They often will let slip more in your presence than mine."

November wasn't a month where snow was uncommon and neither were downright freezing temperatures at night. Just that morning, one of the men had his small toe removed by their surgeon, else infection spoil his blood.

"They are eager to beat the English." Noah plucked up a piece of tall grass to scrape over his teeth.

"Aye. Are not we all?" Brody followed suit, missing the minted powder and cinnamon sticks that he usually used to clean his teeth.

Noah grunted. "And to return north."

Now it was Brody's turn to grunt. He'd been gone from his wife for several weeks and although she was no more than that in name, he found that he did miss her. They hardly knew one another, but every time he'd spoken to her, his soul seemed to reach out to her, sharing things he didn't share with anyone else. The length of time they'd been acquainted with each other didn't matter. Sometimes there were people that simply clicked, for whatever reason. And, shame as it was given her English heritage, he was pretty certain that was the case with the both of them. Her face danced before his closed eyes at night and her smile enchanted him to wake in the morning. She seemed to be the healing balm he needed to heal his wounded heart, even though he was hundreds of miles away from her.

Och, but it would be a long winter without the company of a woman in his bed. The warmth of the one woman who seemed to have garnered all of his attention. Every camp follower, every lightskirt who offered, he had no interest in. There was only one lass he wanted to share an intimate moment with, and that was Guinevere. And the one female he had no chance of having any time soon. Even if he was back at Dunnottar, honor bade him wait as he'd promised. Aye, he'd thought once that he might be able to seduce her, to convince her otherwise, but not anymore. Not now that he felt closer to her.

Brody breathed in a deep breath, grinning up at the trees empty of leaves, boots mired in muck, hundreds of miles from home. Despite his current situation, he had a smile on his face, because he was alive, he still had all his toes, and dammit, but their men were making progress.

By the time Brody and Noah had met up with the men just over a week ago, they'd already taken Berwick-upon-Tweed back into Scottish hands, but had not yet moved beyond the border.

Now they were well into Northumberland, they'd already sacking the villages of Yeavering, Akeld, burning Felton Mill, and nearly ravaged a kirk at the former as well as the men of God who lived there, only stopping from repeating the English's heinous crimes at Dunnottar when Brody pointed out they were behaving exactly the same way—that they'd already had their revenge where a kirk was involved. Wallace had been quick to come to his senses, but the men, thousands of them, were not as easy to convince. The rage that filled them, the self-righteousness... Well, 'twas a good thing several clergymen traveled with the camp, in order to receive the confession of the men, their murderous thoughts, as well as their sins. They'd scorched villages, crops, desecrated the land, murdered, maimed and raped. It was enough to turn

Brody's stomach—and had many nights when he claimed simply to have partaken too much in the plentiful whisky.

In every woman he saw his sisters, his mother, Guinevere and her ladies. More than once he'd ripped a heaving warrior from the prone body of a woman. More than once he'd wrenched a man's shirt from his body and given it to a poor lass to cover her nakedness. Brody was becoming known amongst the warriors as a guardian of virtue and while some who were able to slake their lust with a willing woman, those who preferred the brutal route were angry. Several had challenged him and several had limped back to their tents. Brody could not be beaten.

While some of the men in the vast army had taken liberties with women, had murdered children, Brody forbade his men from participating. No woman would be had by a man under his command unless she was willing. No child would be harmed. No elderly or ill person would be maimed or murdered. If an able-bodied warrior got down on his knees and raised his hands in surrender, he was to be brought before Brody or Noah and only then would his judgment be placed—nevertheless, this was easier to say when a village was seized, but not so on the field of battle. On the field of battle, a man only saw red. The blind rage and bloodlust was needed to dispatch of one's enemy. The pure animal instinct to survive, to fight until your heart no longer beat. Some men, so enmeshed in battle would often find themselves face to face with a warrior they'd spent years of their lives training with, only to not recognize him for who he was.

In that instant, when a man's only order was to survive, to defeat his enemy, it was hard to weed through the red and see what was right in front of him.

They would conduct their raiding with as much honor as they could or suffer the consequences—forty lashes and zero rations for three days.

His men were in full agreement.

Their ultimate goal in the next few days before moving onward was sacking Newcastle Keep and taking its constable as a prisoner. To take the castle was to take the strategic town away from the English. To gut Longshanks where it hurt, as he'd done to them. And most obviously, to have a Scottish stronghold in northern England.

Brody pulled his boots from the mud with a sucking sound. His good leather were caked in at least an inch of thick sludge. Ballocks, but that was going to be a beast of trouble getting clean.

Perhaps if he simply left them caked the mud would provide extra insulation. Prevent him from losing a toe. Might be worth giving it a go. He'd rather save his energy, or that of his squire, for fighting. For staying warm.

Brody trudged back into the camp circle where his horse was tethered. Thunder grazed on what little grass he could find, having emptied the bucket of oats that Brody's squire had fed him. The magnificent warhorse raised his head in greeting, giving a short neigh, before returning to his veritable feast.

"Meat, my laird?"

Brody glanced up to see his squire, Jae, standing there, a hunk of unknown meat on a skewer. Likely a squirrel or rabbit. Fresh meat was rare to come by at camp and he wasn't one to scorn food when hunger filled his belly. But still, he had to ask, "Have ye eaten?" to the young lad, because he believed in feeding his men first.

165

"Aye, my laird." Jay rubbed his belly. "Quite full now."

Brody nodded to the lad and scrubbed a hand over Thunder's muzzle. "Get some rest. We're likely to leave camp come morning."

"Aye, my laird." Jae handed him the long stick of meat.

Brody settled on his rolled out plaid and ate his meat until his belly quit rumbling, then tossed the stick toward the flames. Hands behind his head, he quickly fell into a deep sleep, only to be woken in what felt like moments later by a bell tolling.

Wallace was laughing and standing in the center of camp, banging on a pot—not a bell. Mud streaked his face and his eyes were wild. Hair plaited in braids and pulled to the back of his head. He danced a small jig and continued to bang on the pot until nearly everyone had woken.

Brody rubbed his eyes and stood, shaking the sleep from his body.

"Today we go to Hexham Priory!" Wallace shouted, banging some more on the pot, getting the men riled. They picked up their swords and waved them in the air. "We will hold the English monks for ransom. We will show them mercy where the bastards showed us none!"

Brody's skin prickled. Another place of worship. Wallace couldn't seem to get away from it. As though, perhaps, he thought to hurt them where it hurt the most. A man's devotion to his God was sacred, and the place he worshipped, the men with a connection to the holy, untouchable. Except, it did not appear to be so with this war. He could understand the tactic behind it, even if he didn't agree. Hitting a man where it hurt the most, the place most likely to tear him down, that was how a war was won.

And Wallace had said that his plan was to take the priory hostage. That was a world of difference compared to burning the English in the church. Brody was exceedingly proud of their leader. Wallace had come a long way from wanting only bloodshed, though that was still a priority to him.

The men shouted their excitement, banging on cups and pots and anything that might make a sound. They were quick to clean up camp, rushing here and there to gather their supplies. Loading horses.

Just as they were preparing to leave, one of the men he'd left at Dunnottar rode into camp, covered in sweat and dust from the road.

Brody leapt from his horse and ran to the guard as he climbed from his own mount.

"What's happened?" Brody asked.

"A letter from Lady Keith," the messenger said, out of breath. He reached into his sleeve and pulled out a thick square of parchment.

"The castle is secure?" Brody asked.

"Aye."

"Ye have only come with a letter? No news?"

The messenger looked worried and shook his head. "Her ladyship bade me deliver this to ye and to bring news in return to her."

Brody frowned. That was odd. News from the castle should have only arrived if there was a problem.

"But there is nothing wrong?" Brody asked again to be certain, not truly thinking his guard would lie about such.

"The seneschal has done as ye bade, my laird. The walls are secure, the villagers continuing to pay their tithes and allegiance. Construction continues as planned."

Again Brody frowned, confused. He grunted and tucked the letter up his sleeve. If there was nothing wrong, then why a missive? Perhaps the worrisome news was not fit for the guard's ear.

"We are moving out. Come with us."

There was no time to read her letter just yet and Brody wanted to give the missive its due attention. What on earth could the lass want? Perhaps all was well on the surface but she had concerns of another nature? Och, but was she with child? Her previous husband's bairn? Would Brody have to raise an English arsehole's offspring?

They rode out of camp, his mind a jumble of what could be in the letter. But soon, when they reached the priory, he was met with another contender for his attention.

The stone walls surrounding the priory were sturdy, a bell steeple seen rising from the center of the grounds. Farmlands surrounded the walls, but instead of seeing monks at work, an English army stood at attention just outside the gate.

"Halt!" An English lord, covered in mail, sat tall upon his horse in front of the priory, with perhaps fifty men behind him.

"Ye are heavily outnumbered," Brody called. "Surrender and we may yet let ye live."

Wallace looked at him and frowned—he hated to leave loose ends.

Brody nodded, letting his leader know he had a plan.

"We cannot let you pass," the English lord said, pulling out his sword.

What in bloody hell? Did the man have a death wish? Fifty against thousands? Brody held out his arms, indicating the men behind him. "We have no need for your permission, old man."

The English lord frowned. "Then perhaps we can negotiate."

"We dinna negotiate with the English," Wallace shouted.

"I am the Lord of Arundel, I wish to make a bargain with you."

Lord Arundel... Why did that name sound familiar?

Before Wallace could answer in words that would only lead to battle, Brody hurried ahead. "We will hear your terms, but we cannot guarantee we will heed them."

Lord Arundel lowered his sword, however he didn't sheathe it. "My daughter, she was married to Baron de Ros. Your men took his castle, Dunnottar."

"*Our* castle!" Wallace bellowed. "'Twas never yours! Ye English crossed onto our lands and stole it."

Lord Arundel gave a curt nod acknowledging that truth. "He and his men were killed."

"Justice served!" Wallace shouted again.

"I will not discuss justice with a madman," Lord of Arundel shouted, in return, his face turning red and splotchy with anger. "I want my daughter back."

Brody's blood ran cold.

"Who is your daughter?" he asked, praying it was one of the three ladies who served his wife. Let it even be one of the two who he'd arranged safe passage back to England. Anyone but—

"Lady Guinevere."

"Shite," Wallace ground out, the exact sentiment Brody felt.

They both turned at the same time to eye each other.

169

"This will not go over well," Wallace murmured. "He will want your head."

"He canna have it."

Wallace grimaced.

"My daughter!" Lord Arundel bellowed. "I demand her return."

"Ye canna have her," Brody answered through his bared teeth.

"Then I will not allow you to pass." The man bristled on his horse, his cheeks flaming purple now with anger. His charged shifted restlessly, irritated at how the knight must have been clutching tighter to its middle.

Brody ground his teeth. Och, but if the man was anyone else he'd cut him down. But Lord Arundel was his wife's father. If he ever hoped to find a modicum of peace with her, killing her father in battle would not accomplish that.

"Surrender and we will let ye see your daughter," Brody said.

"Where is she?" Lord Arundel demanded.

Brody cleared his throat. "She is safe."

"Not good enough." Arundel shook his head. "I must know where she is."

"Men on death's door can make no demands," Wallace warned, dragging his own claymore from the sheath on his back.

Several of the earl's men drew their weapons. If Brody didn't calm the atmosphere soon, there would be bloodshed.

"Lay down your arms," Brody commanded. "We will not leave and we will be taking the priory today. As a token of our goodwill, we'll allow ye to send your men back to your king with a message, and I'll take ye to see your daughter myself."

Lord Arundel seemed to ponder this a moment, then nodded. "What is your message?"

Wallace pulled a rolled scroll from his sleeve and nudged his horse forward. He spoke in low tones to the lord, who passed the scroll to a man at his right, stating the Scottish demands for the return of the priory. Coin, supplies, Newcastle Keep.

"Ye're lucky to be left breathing," Wallace said to the earl, as the fifty Arundel knights marched away with the message to Longshanks. "Ye have your son-in-law to thank for that."

Arundel bared his teeth. "De Ros is dead. I'll not be able to thank him for anything."

Wallace laughed and Brody felt his stomach tie into knots, a feeling he'd not had since he was a wee lad. Dear God, but he knew what was coming next and there was no way to stop it.

"Och, my lord, but your son-in-law, he stands before ye now." Wallace grinned from ear to ear at Brody.

Brody could have punched him. Would have if he'd not been the leader of the rebellion and the only man with ballocks big enough to take on the English.

The glower Lord Arundel sent his way was murderous. He shook his head violently. "Nay. Nay. This cannot be."

Brody straightened in his saddle and nodded. "We've been wed for nigh on a month now. In time, ye'll thank me for it, just as she has."

171

CHAPTER FIFTEEN

An entire two weeks passed, and in that time, Guinevere mended at least thirty shirts, fifteen infant gowns and seventy-five pairs of hose. Her basket of children's blankets had doubled in number, too. Not to mention that she'd refreshed the rushes in the great hall and started a new tapestry for the kirk that should be finished within a few months' time. This kirk made entirely from stone, save for the roof.

And in all that time, there was no return letter from Brody.

Not that she'd expected one quite so soon. He was likely at the border and she prayed not in England itself, though she knew such a prayer was naïve. He'd told her he was going there. She should absolutely believe him.

There were any number of reasons why she might not have heard a word back from her husband. In the time since she'd sent the letter, the first dusting of snow covered the ground, which only delayed the work on the castle outside for a few hours while the sun melted what the night had brought. She imagined it would make traveling for the messenger hard, too.

Unable to stand another minute of being cooped up inside, Guinevere insisted on taking a turn about the bailey with the seneschal as he explained the lowered provisions and the reason behind his need to order a one time tithe from the clansmen to stock the storehouses for winter. It felt good to be outside. She wore her fur-lined mantle around her shoulders, not using the hood, and allowed the crisp air to rifle her hair a little bit, to cool her cheeks.

All the while, one ear was keen for any calls of a messenger. It just so happened, as she agreed with the seneschal's plan as long as it did not cause any clansman to starve, the guards atop the gate tower called a friendly greeting to someone.

The seneschal's attention was garnered by the gate and she pretended to follow him for the sake of finishing their conversation. In fact, she wanted to see if it was her messenger returned.

Oh, how nervous she was! Her heart pounded a staccato beat, thundering through her chest and skull. Her mouth was suddenly dry, tongue swollen. Hands shaking, spine trickling a single drop of sweat.

The gate was opened and in rode the messenger she'd been waiting for. He nodded greetings to the men and then searched her out, locking eyes with her.

The messenger dismounted and approached. "My lady." He bowed low and handed her a rolled missive from inside his sleeve.

"Thank you. Any news?" She kept her voice calm, trying not to let her excitement show.

"Aye, what news from the Marischal?" the seneschal asked.

"They are in Northumberland." The messenger kept his gaze steady on her when he relayed the news and she feared he worried she might faint at hearing her husband was no longer in Scotland. "They've sacked several cities. The English run when they hear of their impending arrival."

Guinevere grimaced. Northumberland. Her father was there. Oh, but she prayed that her family was well.

"He has suffered no illness or injury?"

The messenger crossed himself. "Nay, madam."

Guinevere clutched tight to the missive in her hands. She needed to go read the contents immediately.

"That is good news," she said. "Please, go and find something warm to eat, I'm certain your journey was overlong, but please know how much I appreciate it. If you'll excuse me."

The men mumbled something, she couldn't be certain what, and she didn't care.

Brody had written her back.

Why she felt so surprised she wasn't certain. But surprised she was.

Enormously so.

Guinevere hurried into the keep and started for the stairs to her chamber, but then thought better of it. If she went up there, then she'd have to speak with Elinor about the letter, and as much as she loved her dear friend, she wanted a moment of privacy with her husband—well, his letter at least. What if all he'd written was a small, mundane line? What if he rebuked her? Said he wanted an annulment? What if he couldn't read and write? Oh, saints, but she'd not thought of that possibility.

All of these worries only intensified her conclusion that 'twas better to read it in private.

At the second level, she veered off toward the library and barred the door behind her. The room was dark and drafty, barely any light filtered through the slim windows. Guinevere approached an arrow-slit and leaned her back to the windowsill as she ran her fingernail beneath the wax of his seal—two swords crisscrossed.

Slowly, she unrolled the missive, revealing more than a few lines of writing in long sloping scrolls.

My dear lady,

Your letter found me very well, though I daresay we have the messenger you sent to thank for that. All teasing aside, I am well and touched at your concern. I sincerely hope that all is well with you and your lady, and that the other two have found their way safely back to their homes in England.

The weather here is horrid. How did you stand it? We've had nothing but rain and I've given up on cleaning my boots. (I jest, as we have much the same in Scotland!) My boots now have a thick layer of mud insulating them. A good way to stay warm, since you asked. We have plenty of thick plaids, warmed hearth stones, and the crush of bodies—some men prefer the warmth of our female camp followers, but I assure you I am not one of them. Our horses keep us warm when we ride. 'Tis not yet overly freezing. We are men. We manage.

For now, we have made camp at a priory, and before you put your hands on your hips, rest assured, I made certain not a single man was harmed.

The sachet you sent smells heavenly. It reminds me of you. I've kept it rolled in my sleeve and think of you every time I catch its lustrous scent. The men are jealous. I am a lucky man to have a woman think of such a thing as scent when our camp smells of bodily stenches, waste and other such things too vulgar for your tastes.

We have plenty of blankets and hose, but if you are so willing, perhaps a few more sachets? Noah, in particular, continues to sniff my arm like a bloodhound.

Do not fash over your parting words, or mine. Despite your wish to see me dead, I live and breath, and am heartier than ever—and please read this with a smile, perhaps even a laugh. I remember the sound of it, and while I only heard it once or twice, I would very much like to hear it again.

Though I've had family at home to think about me, pray for me, there is something profoundly different in having a wife. And make no mistake, you are mine. I dare not admit this aloud, but each ensuing battle creates in me a lust to return home. To you.

The door? A test? What do you mean? If you are asking if I should require you to fix more doors, the answer is nay, though I will commend you once more on a job well done— and remind you that it was not I who demanded you fix it. You took up that torch on your own. How are your little wounds healing?

I was called away sooner than expected, and I do apologize for that. This does not mean that I am breaking my promise, only that we seem to be delayed in getting started. I've not had a letter from a woman other than my mother before now, nor have I written one. I find it humorous that at thirty and two, I have found something new. I admit—another admission, why do I feel you are so easy to confide in?—that I rather like the idea of writing to you. Perhaps, though we are apart, we can learn more about each other through the written word.

Tell me, iasg beag, *what would your family think if they found out we two were married?*

Your Honorable Husband

For never having received a letter from a woman not his mother, nor written one, Brody did a fine job. His handwriting was neat and legible. His content jovial and she could hear his voice, feel him near her just from reading it.

Guinevere clutched the letter to her chest, having a hard time wrapping her head around the fact that he'd written her at all—and at length. That he wanted to get to know her.

It wasn't until now, reading his letter, that she realized she'd not actually expected to receive a reply.

How thrilling!

In person, Brody was nothing short of a brusque warrior. A man of steel and power. She anticipated him lopping off her head more than sending her such a long and detailed letter. One in which she felt his... concern? Care? Perhaps even the beginning of a well-formed friendship?

And yet, when he'd mentioned the men taking women to bed, felt compelled to tell her he was faithful, it had startled her. Taken her breath. Many husbands took mistresses and most men took women to bed when they were at war. But not Brody.

Was it too much, too whimsical, to wonder if he was saving himself for her? She couldn't imagine that a man such as him was a virgin. There was no possible way. Guinevere laughed at her girlish fancies. She was reading too much into his words. He'd simply been kind enough—as he'd been since the moment he promised himself to her—to tell her that he was not taking a lover. He would respect their bonds of marriage.

Even the way he'd signed the letter, *Honorable*, he was proclaiming his intentions.

Either the man was a very good liar, or she'd managed to find the one and only man in all of Christendom who was worth a damn.

He wanted to hear her laugh.

Wanted to see her again.

Why did that have to make her heart rush? Why did that cause her breath to falter?

Was it possible that despite her initial desires of finding a way to escape this man, this marriage, that she… liked him? Perhaps a little more than she'd originally thought?

Nay. Nay. Nay.

Oh, but *aye*. She did.

He was kind and funny. Handsome and strong. Honorable. Desirable.

Guinevere swallowed the lump that had formed in her throat.

As odd as it may be, perhaps she should take to heart his request to learn more about each other from letters. So that when he returned home, she'd know for certain whether or not she wanted to be there.

She rushed to the desk, intent on writing a return letter, but could only find a small scrap of parchment inside one of the drawers and no other larger pieces upon the shelves or within the wardrobe.

No matter, she'd not let the size of the parchment keep her from writing him.

Dear, most honorable husband,

First, I must apologize for the tiny scrap of parchment and the smallness of my words. I find myself too eager to return your letter to search out a larger piece. I was beyond thrilled to receive it. I was not certain one would ever arrive. And to know that you and the men are alive is a balm to my soul. I will continue to pray for you, though I must admit, I pray for my countrymen as well. My sisters, my family.

As you mentioned them, I must say I am not certain their enthusiasm would be great. My three sisters would be horrified. And I'm afraid they might end up in ill health if they knew. Their dispositions being much like Abigail and Claudia. My mother, whom I'm told I take after, would try and find the good in it, if only to help my sisters and my father to come to terms.

My father serves King Edward and will be displeased to find out I've married the man responsible in part for de Ros' death. But, beneath that ire, perhaps he will be pleased to know that you saved me. That you promised me protection.

179

I did write to them, to tell them I was safe. Though I failed to mention we'd wed. I confess my decision on this was because I did not wish my father to bring war to Dunnottar. The people here have suffered enough, and if withholding a truth for a little while could keep it that way, then alas, I am bound to see it done as their mistress.

Tell me, Marischal, what of your family? Will they be displeased?

How long will you be at the priory? Will you winter there? The seneschal seems to think the kirk will be completed before the first real snow, though we've had a dusting already. You should see the improvements. If I were decent at drawing, I'd draw you a picture. Alas, my skills at artistry are only with a needle.

I have already two dozen sachets prepared and your messenger should have them, though I know this will not be enough, so I will make more and have them sent with haste.

And once more she found herself struggling with how to sign her letter. Guinevere chewed her lip. He'd claimed himself honorable in his signature. What should she claim to be? What *was* she? For certes, she, too, was honorable. But she was also loyal, mostly, and anxiously awaiting the end of the war. And then she knew, the perfect word to convey just what he should think of her. A combination of loyal, honorable, dependable. Constant. For she would wait. If only in the end to drive a dagger through his heart herself if he only offered betrayal.

Your trustworthy wife,
Lady Guinevere

Chapter Sixteen

"Where is General Gray?" Brody crossed his arms over his chest and stared down at Lord Arundel who sat, stripped of his weapons, in a chair inside the small chamber they'd deemed to be his cell during their short stay at the priory.

The walls were bare save for three hooks to hang a monk's clothes. A small cot sat against the wall, with a short and narrow shelf. The only other pieces of furniture were a small table and this very chair.

Arundel's lip quivered, the beginnings of a smile. "Scotland."

Brody narrowed his gaze, flexing his hands in an effort to still himself from hitting the man. "Where in Scotland?"

Arundel grinned slowly, the same deliberate flash of teeth he'd been casting since they'd taken him into custody the week before. A knowing, pain in the arse smile. And still no answers.

The bastard had already gleaned that Brody would not harm his daughter, so what more upper hand could Brody have? The man's own life? Nay, Arundel had already decided that would be on the line when he was knighted thirty some odd years prior. At least that's what he said when Brody asked if he wanted to die.

Brody wasn't against torture to get the answers he needed, but there was something holding him back. Guinevere.

Even Wallace thought it wouldn't be a good idea to threaten the man with a beating or missing fingers or toes. He'd probably already come to the conclusion that he wouldn't be going home. Or maybe he even assumed they would kill him anyway.

They'd searched through Arundel's things and found nothing of value. The man had given up no answers, save for just now saying Gray was in Scotland

The men in Arundel's army had gone off to the king and returned with an army of greater size, but that had still not been enough to thwart the Scots from their intent. They continued their local attacks, using the priory as their base.

The English continued to come in waves, which in the end kept the Scottish army from their ultimate destination—Newcastle. Wallace was on the verge of snapping in his frustration.

"Is General Gray headed back to Stirling?" Brody asked for the hundredth time. They'd gotten word Longshanks would try to take back the castle at some point. If Arundel was admitting Gray was back in Scotland, then Brody's guess would be that was where he was headed.

Arundel sat forward, his eyes locked on Brody's. "Why do you care so much about Gray?"

Brody laughed. "Trust me when I say, we care about all the generals in Edward's army."

Arundel shook his head. "Nay. There is something more about Gray. Something personal. Your eyes, they change when you say his name."

"Ye're mistaken." Brody relaxed, kept his face from giving away what he truly felt toward the raping, murdering, bastard Gray. The hatred that burned in his blood every time he said the man's name. "I've never met the man a day in my life." And that was true. By the time he'd fought his way through the English army at his keep, the general and his lot had run off, leaving his sister's prone form, and his father's lasts words, "*Gray... General Gray...*"

Arundel grunted. "Mayhap, but that doesn't change what I know."

Brody ground his teeth. Arundel was baiting him. Trying to get him to give something away. He wouldn't reveal a damned thing to this man, no matter his relation to Guinevere.

"Your silence is telling," Arundel continued to mock him, smiling as though he were a cat who'd just caught a fat, juicy mouse.

Brody swung around, slamming his hands down on the arm of the man's chair, rattling the wood. He brought his face within inches of the older man and snarled. "Ye do realize that your daughter's life is in my hands, do ye not? That your verra bloodline will mingle with mine? That your grandchild will have the same accent as I do, and wear plaid, and hate the bloody English as much as any true Scot?"

His venomous words had the intended effect. Anger brewed in Arundel's eyes. His face turned purple again and his lips white, they were stretched so thin around his bared teeth.

"You're a savage." Spittle formed on the man's lips.

"Savage, barbarian, monster, whatever ye like to call it, but know this, your daughter, your precious Guinevere, is my wife. Linked to me for all time."

To this, Arundel smirked, jerking forward himself. "So you think."

Brody grabbed the man by his throat, momentarily lost in his sense of rage. "So I *know*."

Arundel garbled a laugh, his face turning red from lack of oxygen. He croaked out, "You and your army will go down in flames—after we gut you like the beasts that you are."

Brody thrust the man away from him, rage, molten hot, running through his veins. He turned his back on Arundel, needing air. Storming from the room, he nearly ripped the door from its hinges, then growled to the guard outside, "No food or water for three days. Unless he tells us where Gray is."

By the third day, if Arundel still wasn't talking, then the man was willing to die to keep his secrets and there was nothing Brody or anyone could do about it.

Brody burst out into the priory courtyard, muscles tight, breath flaming, just as a messenger arrived.

"Chief," he said, dismounting.

Brody tried not to glower at the man, but it was hard to rid himself of the anger so quickly.

"Is aught amiss?" the messenger asked, stopping in his tracks.

"What is it?" Brody growled, ignoring his question.

"A letter and a package from Dunnottar."

Brody took them both, the scents from the bundle calming him. "Give these to Noah. Tell him to disperse them to the injured men."

There weren't many of them, but those who lay ill, surrounded by the scents of it, deserved some sweetness first.

"Aye, chief." The messenger ran off, leaving Brody with his anger and the tiny scroll in his hand.

Brody marched toward the nave, intent on privacy. When they'd taken the priory hostage, he'd chosen not to have a private cell of his own in favor of staying with his men. Aye, he was their leader, but he was also one of them. If they were all to sleep on the hard, wintry grounds for months, then so was he.

Once in the nave, he slipped into shadows, hidden from view, but not so much that he couldn't see the contents of the opened letter.

Brody had to keep himself from laughing aloud at her polite words—her father would be displeased. The man was spitting mad. Ready to commit murder should he be let loose.

Exactly the reason Arundel had been restrained in his cell. He'd attacked one of the guards that morning, having forgotten his agreement to be taken hostage apparently.

Reading his wife's words gave him a sense of calm. One he wouldn't have expected. She was sweet, endearing, and honest.

185

Her closing—*trustworthy*—saints, but she wouldn't have known how much he needed to know that. How much that would mean to him.

Without being at Dunnottar himself, he worried incessantly over whether or not she was safe, the holding was safe, his people. Aye, he was doing good for the country now, but he wasn't even in it.

England was a dreary place, and the more time that passed, the more he was certain they'd be driven back. He hated being in Longshanks' country. They'd been able to sack several small towns, but not yet had they been able to take a more significant castle.

They needed more men. More strategy. The English, bastards though they happened to be, were prepared. Had been waiting for just such an invasion.

And Arundel... No wonder he doubted Brody's threats. Now he knew why the man doubted whether Brody was married to Guinevere, for she'd written her family and assured them of her safety, but not told them.

Ballocks.

This entire time he'd been bartering something the man did not believe in. Aye, he knew his daughter was still at Dunnottar, but not that they'd wed. Perhaps he thought she was a prisoner. So, why had he agreed to stay at the priory? What was he doing here, biding his time? Offering himself up in exchange for her?

Well, this was all the proof he needed to show that they were truly wedded, to get the man talking about Gray.

Brody stormed back toward the dormitories and Arundel's cell. He pushed past the guard, thrusting himself through the door.

Arundel's head snapped up, a smirk on his face.

Brody brandished the letter, waving it in front of the man's face.

"Recognize the handwriting? 'Tis a letter from my wife."

Arundel blanched, writhing in the chair. "Let me see that," he growled.

Brody held the letter steady so the man could take a good look at the handwriting and the signature on the bottom.

"I feel obliged to read this aloud to ye, ye bloody fool. The letter I just received from my wife—your daughter." Brody cleared his throat. "*I did write to them, to tell them I was safe. Though I failed to mention we'd wed. I confess my decision on this was because I did not wish my father to bring war to Dunnottar. The people here have suffered enough, and if withholding a truth for a little while could keep it that way, then alas, I am bound to see it done as their mistress.*"

Arundel shook his head ferociously. "'Tis a forgery. A lie!"

"If ye wish to believe that, then so be it. But how would I know that she'd sent ye a letter at all, let alone the contents in order to create such a forgery?"

"A guess!"

Brody laughed. "Come, fool, ye dinna think me so unwise as to hazard a guess that could jeopardize everything, do ye? And if ye do, then more a fool ye." His expression turned serious. Deadly. "For I have married your daughter. Her verra life is in my hands."

Arundel's lips curled up over his teeth. "You need to leave England. Now."

Brody shook his head. "Even with her life on the line ye would continue making threats?"

"You don't understand." Arundel shook his strapped down arms and let out an angry bellow. "Guinevere is in danger."

Brody narrowed his eyes. "What do ye mean by that? What have ye done?"

"When my men left me here, they sent an order to General Gray."

Now it was Brody's turn to blanch, his blood running cold.

"Dinna stop speaking on my account." Brody's tone was deadly and he reached for the sword at his hip.

"General Gray would have left to go to Dunnottar, to avenge the English, and to bring my daughter back to England." Arundel was writhing in earnest now. "We need to leave."

Would Guinevere go with Gray? Brody could hardly breathe. He'd not known her long, but even still, in their fragile relationship, a bond had formed. He didn't want to lose her.

Arundel slammed his fists as much as he could tied up, on the chair arms. "If that truly is her letter, and she sees herself as mistress, accepts her position as your wife, then she will not let the English take the castle. She will fight."

Brody swallowed. Arundel didn't need to say more. Guinevere was stubborn, protective. Brody knew what General Gray was capable of. What he'd do to a woman who chose to fight. He'd not honor Arundel's request to bring Guinevere back to England. He'd make up a lie, that she was already dead or escaped, and he'd rape her. Brutally. Repeatedly. Just as he'd done to poor Johanna and countless others. Only, perhaps his treatment of her would be worse, because he'd want to punish her for trying to fight against him.

"If anything should happen to her, 'twill be on your head," Brody said coolly, stabbing his finger toward the earl. "And I will be the one to take it."

"I am not the only one to blame. You left her alone."

There was more truth in that than Brody was willing admit. So, instead, he let his fist fly, dealing the English lord, his father-by-marriage, a blow he'd been waiting over a week to dish out.

Arundel's chair tumbled backward. Brody didn't bother to help break his fall or lift him back up. He did, however, resist the urge to spit on the man, to leap on top of him and hit him again.

The guard outside the door flung it open, worry on his face. "Marischal?"

Brody bristled, gritting his teeth. "Help the bastard up. We're leaving. Now."

"Aye, my laird."

Brody rushed to the cloister, in search of Noah or Wallace or both. He found them huddled together in the room Wallace had taken over to draw his maps and plot out his strategies against the English.

"Wallace, Noah." The two men shot their heads up, immediately taking note of his wretched face.

"What's happened?"

"Who died?"

Brody's fingers went from tingly to numb. "Arundel confessed the whereabouts of Gray. He's taken an army to Dunnottar."

"Bloody hell," Wallace said.

"Ye know the history between Gray and my family," Brody said. "I have to go. My wife's life is in danger."

"Aye. Go," Wallace said.

"I'll go with ye," Noah said.

"Nay, ye stay," Brody said. "Ye're needed here."

"I would be by your side. I loved Johanna and your father, too." Noah had a point, a stake in this fight, and Brody agreed.

"Go, the both of ye," Wallace said. "Kick some English arse. Keeping the castle we just took back from them is as important as what we're doing here."

The two of them nodded and rushed from the room, preparing the men to depart. Brody didn't know the size of Gray's army and he didn't care. The man could have ten thousand and Brody would see him burned alive before he was through.

They were gone from the priory within an hour, riding hard north, stopping only to let the horses rest, so they were not made lame. Arundel was with them, tied up like a the stuck boar that he was.

If Brody was lucky, they'd arrive at Dunnottar at the same time as the English bastards.

And he'd not let one of them live.

Chapter Seventeen

Guinevere woke with a start, her skin clammy, hands shaking.

Elinor's side of the bed was empty, cold. Her maid must have risen at least an hour before and not woken her.

But it was still dark out. Through the shutters, no light filtered, and the fire in the hearth was not yet banked.

They'd probably only closed their eyes mayhap a few hours before.

What had woken her?

A night terror she couldn't remember?

"Elinor?" Guinevere shifted her feet over the side of the bed, pushing her blankets away that tangled around her waist.

There was no answering call, but she swore she could hear voices beyond the chamber door that combined their two rooms. Was Elinor entertaining a guest?

It was no secret that her friend enjoyed the companionship of men, 'twas one of the reasons she'd been able to find out so much information around the castle that she then relayed back to Guinevere. She'd tried to talk to her about it once, but Elinor made it clear she was not doing anything that would ruin her reputation. Or at least that was the claim she stood by.

But in the dead of night?

Something didn't sit right.

The hairs on the back of Guinevere's neck prickled and a sudden silence reigned from beyond the connecting door.

Dear God in Heaven… Why was she so afraid?

Her gut told her something was wrong and yet the logical side of herself said there couldn't be. That they had five hundred of Brody's soldiers and a high, thick wall. No one could breach it. And yet, Brody had. And her husband had before him. Tingles rained over her scalp. If her instincts were on fire, then something had to be amiss. And if she found out that she simply had an overactive imagination, all the better.

Guinevere tiptoed to the hearth and gripped the fire poker before approaching the door. She listened, not hearing anything, but still silence filled the air. Had her imagination been playing tricks on her? 'Twas possible that Elinor had simply gone to the privy, or maybe sought to sleep in her own chamber because Guinevere had been snoring, which she did do on occasion.

She touched her fingers to the door handle, but then quickly pulled back. What if Elinor *was* entertaining a man, despite never having done so this late before? Guinevere didn't want to walk in on that. Such a private moment she herself had never actually encountered…

Unless, of course, they were simply talking?

But talking required speaking, of which Guinevere heard no more.

Perhaps her entry would be a good reminder to Elinor to keep herself chaste. Guinevere had warned her that behaving that way would lessen her chances of a good marriage.

Guinevere squeezed her eyes shut in the dark. All right. She'd just open it. Or knock.

Nay, because if she knocked and there was an intruder, it would only alert him she was coming. Then again, hadn't she basically done that already when she called her friend's name a moment ago?

Aye.

So they would already be expecting her. Well, enough with the contemplations. She could stand here deliberating what to do for hours.

She lifted her hand again, prepared to open the door when it sprung open.

A face loomed in the dark.

"Mrs. Donald?" Guinevere said, confused, taking in the older woman's visage, her wild, mussed hair. "What are you doing in Elinor's chamber?"

The elderly cook didn't answer, but grabbed Guinevere's arm with pinching and surprisingly strong fingers, yanking her forward.

"Ye're not to ask any questions, *Sassenach*."

The way she said it was like a curse, hateful, spiteful. Ugly.

This was not right. Mrs. Donald had never been pleasant to her but… She'd never dared touch her either, or make such verbal threats. Guinevere yanked away, leaping back a step and brandishing the poker in front of her. 'Twas hard to see with only the light of the moon to guide her, but she'd do her best to aim true. To protect herself and her friend.

"Don't touch me! How dare you? Where is Elinor?"

"The bitch is tied up," Mrs. Donald hissed. "Just like ye will be in a minute."

Guinevere was too outraged to be shocked silent. A guttural shout, her own battle cry, ripped from her throat and she lunged forward, thrusting her shoulder into the older woman's chest. Mrs. Donald lost her balance, stumbling backward and falling on her arse. Guinevere searched the room quickly while Mrs. Donald struggled to her feed. But the room was empty.

"Where is she?" she screeched, but Mrs. Donald didn't answer, only charged her like a boar.

Guinevere swung the poker using all her strength, prepared to connect. The poker met her mark, striking Mrs. Donald's arm with a sickening crack.

Mrs. Donald screamed, clutching her arm to her chest. "Ye broke my bloody arm!"

"That is no less than what you deserve for attacking me and my lady. Where is she?"

The cook stumbled back on legs that were no longer so sturdy. "Ye shouldna done that! I'll never tell ye where she is. Rot in hell, ye devil's spawn!"

If the older woman wouldn't talk, then Guinevere would find her lady herself. She darted for the door, tugged it open, and ran straight into a rough, wool sack.

"Gotcha now." The voice was Scottish, but not one she could immediately recognize.

He tugged the sack over her head and as she fought him, he knocked the poker from her hand and wrapped his arms tight around her to keep her from fighting.

"She broke my arm, Toby," Mrs. Donald called behind. "No need to coddle the bitch. Mayhap she takes a stumble on the stairs afore she reaches that English lord. He did say if she was already dead he didna care."

"But he said the reward would be doubly sweet if she was alive. And, since we're going against the Marischal, I want more coin for doing so."

Guinevere fought against the sack, screaming out, "Help!" but it would seem all for naught. Her voice was muffled and no one came to her aid.

Had the whole castle turned against her?

If only she'd gone home with Abigail and Claudia. Escaped when she had the chance. How stupid had she been to think she could make a life with Brody when his whole country hated the English?

"Let me go, you fools! The Marischal will have your heads for this!"

But her threats only made them laugh. "He'll be thanking us is what he'll be doing, whore, if he ever returns home, and if he ever finds us."

Toby lifted her, tossing her over his bony shoulder and knocking the wind from her. Guinevere choked, and writhed against him, the sharp point of his shoulder digging into her stomach. Oh, she was going to be sick. This could not be happening. Wake up! Wake up! But her mind only settled into her predicament, making her aware that she was very much awake.

"Go now, afore anyone who has second thoughts comes to her aid," Mrs. Donald said.

Anyone.

Who else was involved? Had they all turned against her?

Tears pricked Guinevere's eyes. She'd spent over a year trying to be kind and continued to do so after marrying Brody. But none of them cared? No one would put themselves between her and her attackers? They hated her that much? And Mrs. Donald, she'd been a servant of Brody's for a long time. Had he put her up to this? Had he managed to draw her close to get her to let down her defenses and truly feel safe, only to have her abducted? Nay! She couldn't believe it. He'd been so genuine with her, how could she even imagine him doing such a thing? Besides, Mrs. Donald had said an English lord was behind it.

"Quit your moving," Toby muttered.

"I'll take care of that," Mrs. Donald said and then there was a sharp pain blasting through Guinevere's skull.

She cried out, her eyes rolling. The fire poker; Mrs. Donald must have hit her with it.

Her tongue went numb first and the pain increased. But she didn't fall asleep as Mrs. Donald likely wanted. She kept quiet though, going as limp as she could, hoping they'd believe it worked and would speak of things they wouldn't had she been awake. *Stay strong. Stay strong. Stay strong.*

"She's out," Toby said.

"Good."

"Where are we to meet the English?"

The English... Who?

"Postern gate. They are going to take their ships home."

"Conniving bastards. Our laird wanted their ships."

"He wanted this chit, too. He'll thank us though, especially for getting rid of the pox-riddled galleons."

"Aye." Toby shifted her on his shoulder as he descended the stairs.

Perhaps the hardest thing she'd ever had to do in her life was remain limp instead of seizing up at the sudden shift. The descent was jarring and more than once, she felt herself sliding off his shoulder only to be wrenched back on. He was a big lad, aye, but he was already shaking beneath her and she feared he'd fall down the stairs under her weight.

Stay still. Stay still. Breathe slow.

Toby took the stairs slowly and, behind him, Mrs. Donald continued to talk, excited and breathless.

"Where did ye put the other chit? The Englishman didn't seem to care about her too much."

"She's locked up in the dungeon. Knocked out cold, she shouldn't scream for hours and when she does, everyone will understand."

"Aye, they will. They'll thank us, too."

Everyone? But, Guinevere thought, hadn't they said earlier that everyone was on their side? She was so confused.

Round and round the circular stair they descended with her growing dizzier by the minute.

"What do ye suppose the Englishman wants with her? He didn't seem too concerned with her well-being." Toby squeezed her legs and, for a second, she feared he'd pat her bottom and she'd not be able to stay silent or still.

197

"Who cares? Get her out of here. Dunnottar, and all of Scotland, has been sullied enough with the English."

"She helped my ma once, ye know, Mrs. Donald. She's not all bad."

"I dinna care about that and neither will your ma. She'll be happy the curse of the English is gone."

Toby grunted and Guinevere tried to remember hearing of the ladies of the villages speaking of a son named Toby. She couldn't. There were so many she'd helped over the past year. Mending clothes, bringing them food, even helping to weed a few personal vegetable gardens. Anything to keep herself occupied.

And look what it had gotten her.

A wound on her head that she was very concerned about—she could feel the blood trickling over her scalp—and an abduction.

"Remember, Toby, I was there. I told ye the story. The master's sister and father, both murdered by the English. Poor, poor, sweet Johanna. His lairdship could barely recognize her after what they did to her. We dinna want them coming back around. Best give them what they want, get rid of all their blood, and no one else of Scottish blood should have to suffer."

Guinevere's heart constricted. So much fell into place with just this bit of information. Brody's hurt and pain. His kindness. His hatred of the English. His compassion for women in need. The mention of sisters and then changing it only to one. This was why he suffered and she wanted to reach out to him, wherever he was, and pull him into her, to hug him and tell him that she was sorry. That she was sorry, though she had nothing to do with it. That she would gladly repent for whatever evil man had done that to his sister. For the death of his father. She'd not yet lost a parent and, miraculously, not a sibling either, but knew when and if she did before the lord called her back to the earth, it would be beyond painful. Soul crushing. Oh, and for Brody, how much more so, given he was a warrior? He would blame himself. He would be forever tormented with not having done enough to save them. Tears pricked Guinevere's eyes. This was why he was so determined when it came to her, he couldn't bear the thought of another woman suffering as his sister did.

"I remember, Mrs. Donald. That's why I'm helping ye. I think 'tis only just that we cleanse the land of them all, not just a few. I only hope they dinna treat their own as they did ours."

Mrs. Donald snorted. "Why should ye care what they do to her? Think she cares what they'd do to ye?"

Toby made a questionable sound.

"Let me assure ye, she doesna."

They reached the bottom of the stairs and Mrs. Donald bade him stop.

"Artair will not be pleased. He's got his head so far up the master's arse, he can taste his supper."

Artair, the seneschal. Guinevere sent up a silent prayer for the man to appear. He always did whenever she was in need, and she'd often wondered if Brody had tasked him with following her.

Alas, he must have been abed, which was not surprising given it was the middle of the night, for he did not appear and Mrs. Donald gave Toby the go ahead to move forward. Moments later, they exited the keep, the chill late autumn air snaking up her nightrail. Goosebumps covered her skin and, for a moment, she wondered if someone who was unconscious could react to cold. But of course they could. Without the appropriate garments to protect her, too long spent exposed to the cold night and she might just freeze to death.

Whether 'twas unconscious or not, Toby rubbed at her cold legs. Perhaps in an effort to warm his own hands, she wasn't certain. She had a feeling if it weren't for Mrs. Donald continually shoving into his brain that she was the enemy, the lad might have tried to help her. His mother had trusted her, and so should he, but Guinevere couldn't point that out without giving away she was awake. Pain spiked continually through her skull and she wasn't certain how much longer she could hold on to consciousness.

The place where Mrs. Donald had hit her with the poker was warm. Sticky. Bleeding. And the way she was draped over Toby's shoulder made the injury pulse. Her lips were numb. Eyes watery. She'd forced herself to keep her eyes open, but more and more they drooped.

They walked for just a short jaunt until Mrs. Donald hissed something to the guards. The sound of a door opening reached her. But not just any door. The postern gate.

And then they were descending once more, her belly slamming into Toby's shoulder one hundred sixty times until they reached the beach.

"The lady," Mrs. Donald said.

"And your silver," came the smooth voice of an Englishman.

Guinevere could place him immediately. The cool, suave tones of General Gray, a man who had given her a chill of warning from the first time she'd met him as a small girl.

This was all starting to make sense. He'd somehow managed to infiltrate the castle through the Scots, paying off Mrs. Donald and countless others into giving Guinevere up.

Betrayed by both Scots and English, it appeared the only person on her side was in another country—her husband.

"You, boy, hand her over. Both of you, go back to the castle and pretend as though nothing has happened. Await my signal in the morning to open the postern gate for my men to infiltrate the castle walls."

She was transferred none too gently and then nearly dropped onto wood that swayed—a boat.

Thank God she knew how to swim, because that may be the only way of getting out of this—if she could remain awake enough to escape.

CHAPTER EIGHTEEN

A mile from Dunnottar, Brody could make out a dozen campfires. The English were here. He held up his hand to stall his men's movement. Having left most of his army with Wallace, when Arundel confessed that that Gray would have one hundred men, he only traveled with seventy-five. They could easily take on two or three English per warrior normally. Seventy-five put them well past the advantage.

They were less than a day behind the English who traveled slower given their heavy armor. They'd tracked their route and avoided every English scout along the way. Surprise was on their side.

The moon was a thin sliver tonight, not affording Brody as much light as he would have wanted, but they'd traversed these grounds more than the English, and he knew the way. Signaling to Noah that he wanted a word in private, the two of them rode slightly ahead. "We'll take them by surprise, surround them before they realize what's happened, and take them all out."

"If they are already here, perhaps since this afternoon, should we not ride ahead to the castle?" Noah asked.

Brody's entire body sizzled with fury. "Ye're right. If my suspicions are correct, he won't be here waiting. The bastard would have gone ahead. Perhaps even tricked the guards by saying he was sent by her father. He'll have left his army here to attack later. Guinevere would have let him in if she recognized him." A cold sweat trickled down Brody's spine. "I'll climb the wall as I did with Wallace. Sneak in before they know anything. They'll hear the battle at their camp, but will not expect me."

"Aye. I'll lead the attack on their camp."

"Save General Gray for me if he is there. I want to be the one to drive my sword through his heart."

"Aye. Ye have my word. Mind if I rough him up a bit?"

"Not at all. If I'm not back by morning, storm the castle and take it back in the Keith name."

"Cousin..."

"Agree." Brody's tone brooked no argument.

"I agree."

Brody nodded. "And my wife, keep her safe. I dinna trust her father. A man that would send such a vile devil as Gray after his own daughter... He canna tell me he didna know of the man's disposition."

"He strikes me as a man verra much into himself. 'Haps he didna notice."

Brody grunted. "I'll not give him the benefit of my doubt."

"Will ye take two men with ye?" Noah asked. "Only so someone has your back."

"No one can climb as fast as me, save Wallace, and he's not here."

"Aye, but they'll catch up."

Brody was of a mind to say nay, but the smartest thing would be to at least have some backup in case Gray had decided to take half his army with him to the castle already.

He signaled to two men, while Noah arranged for scouts to spy on the English's camp. Then he patted his cousin on the back and wished him well.

Just as he and Wallace had done before, he left Thunder with the men and ran the last mile to the castle, slinking down the slope to stay out of sight.

The closer he got, the more concerned he became. The castle itself appeared quiet. The men walked the wall, there wasn't much noise. All looked to be in perfect, peaceful order. Had his assumptions been wrong?

Was it possible that Gray was being cautious and waiting until morning?

Or was this a trap?

When they'd attacked the Keith stronghold in East Lothian, Gray and his army had done so at night. The man was not about to fight fair, why change his tactics now?

Something was off. The hair on the back of Brody's neck prickled and his blood swooshed at heightened speed through his veins.

The men behind him were quiet, waiting, and when Brody stopped to stare up at the wall, he only saw Scots, recognized his cousin, Anderson. If his own men were still manning the gate, there was no need to sneak inside.

Brody grunted and walked right up to the gate. Anderson and the second guard on the gate tower, immediately spotted him.

"My laird?"

"Aye. Let me in. Make haste, but dinna announce me."

Anderson made several hand signals. Two men raised the portcullis and then opened the gate.

When Brody entered, those on watch stared down at him from the battlements as though he were a ghost.

"Where are the rest of the men?" Anderson asked.

"A mile back." Brody studied Anderson, the rest of the guards. They looked very concerned about him, but not about anything within the castle. Mayhap he had returned before Gray had a chance to infiltrate. "Surrounding an English army."

"Bloody hell. I'll rouse the men," Anderson said. "We had no warning."

Brody trusted his cousin. "Nay. Dinna. I have reason to believe that we've already been infiltrated." Anderson looked incredulous. "Man the gate. Everyone act as though nothing is amiss, and whatever ye do, dinna announce my return, in case I am right." To the two warriors he'd brought with him, Brody said, "Quietly search the perimeter of the castle. I'll search inside the keep."

The moment Brody entered the keep, he could feel a difference in the air. Something charged, angry. He grabbed a torch, raced up the stairs to his wife's chamber, bursting through the door and found it exactly as he expected. Empty.

"*Mo chreach*." He stormed across the chamber to the maid's quarters and found her room empty, too, as well as signs of a struggle. The bed was askew, a chair knocked over, the fire poker near the door, droplets of blood near the door.

He was too late.

God save whoever had drawn her blood.

Immediately, he rushed to the corridor and bellowed, sounding an alarm.

Running up to the next level and the next, he searched, not finding her, and knowing he wouldn't anyway. Down he went, round and round, servants rousing. All the while sensing in his gut that she'd not reappear within the walls. Somehow, Gray had managed to slip like a specter through the stone to steal away his wife.

The seneschal rushed to him. "My laird, ye're back. What's happened?"

"My wife is missing."

"Missing? But I saw her at supper." Artair rubbed his silver hair. "No one has come into the castle. No visitors."

"Someone knows something." Brody searched the sea of faces, all filled with sleep and bewilderment.

He shook his head. If not for the signs of struggle, blood on the floor, he might have thought that she'd simply left him. That she'd somehow been in touch with Gray or her father and figured out a way to simply walk out of the castle walls herself.

"Make no mistake, I will find her. If any of ye know something, ye'd do best to speak now."

"My laird!" One of his guards that he'd sent to search the perimeter came rushing into the castle. "A ship, there is a light on it."

"What? I thought they were all dead?" He purposefully asked the Scottish servants who'd been at the castle when the English occupied it.

They all nodded.

"Where is Mrs. Donald?" Brody asked, suddenly realizing she was not present.

"Must still be asleep," a lumbering lad said.

"Who are ye?" Brody asked.

"T-Toby."

"And your position?"

The lad's eyes shifted. "I'm one of the butchers, my laird."

Brody grunted. "Go and find Mrs. Donald."

Toby rushed off, but not in the direction of the kitchens.

"Follow him," Brody said to one of his men. "I'm going to find out why that ship is lit."

The blanket beneath Guinevere's body was grimy and felt damp. It smelled musty, moldy.

She'd been laying there for what felt like hours, but in truth she knew it couldn't have been too long. From the small rowboat, someone had tossed her over their shoulder and climbed a wobbly ladder, on which they cursed the entire way up. Judging from the smell—death, illness, rotting wood—she guessed that she was on one of the English galleons. Perhaps even her own. Someone had tossed her like a sack of grain onto a bed. How ironic would it be, if it was the very one she'd slept in on her original journey to Scotland?

Her head pounded and pain radiated in waves from one temple to the other. It had grown harder and harder to stay awake. The wool sack was still over her head and her breath was hot. The pain was strong enough now that every so often, she found the need to fist her hands into the decaying sheets, clench her teeth and squeeze her eyes shut—and this she did in order to stay awake, rather than succumb to the darkness that promised to be without pain.

At first, she could hear voices in the distance, and then all was quiet.

Still, she didn't feel safe enough to fall asleep. Not with General Gray as her captor. What could he want with her? Nothing good.

If her father had sent him, then he wouldn't have told Mrs. Donald that he didn't care if she was dead or alive.

Nay, Gray had to be working on his own, which left her terrified. How many times had she witnessed him licking his lips and staring at her as though she were a fine roasted piece of meat? Countless, and every time it sent a chill of warning along her spine. She was not safe.

In fact, she should try to escape now that it appeared no one was within shouting distance.

Guinevere raised her arms, trembling hands tugging the wool over her head. 'Twas dark, but the sliver of moon shone through the tiny porthole.

She was, indeed, aboard her own ship, though this cabin had been de Ros'. One of his tunics still hung from a hook on the wall.

Judging from the room, the ship had been left much the same as when they debarked, the scents of rotting though, were new. A ship full of the dead, and ghosts who couldn't maintain it. And the corpses… She prayed not to encounter any as the men had died aboard ship only a few months before.

This ship itself, without having had any upkeep in all those months of being occupied by ill sailors and then the dead, 'twould be dangerous to put it to sea.

Was that a danger General Gray was willing to take? Or did he have a regiment of men willing to put it to use waiting quietly somewhere in the hull?

Guinevere tried to sit up, but the pounding in her head turned into a violent rushing. The room swirled and she leaned over the side of the bed to wretch—as quietly as she could. Acid burned the back of her throat. Her eyes watered and she laid back down.

She touched the place on her head where Mrs. Donald had hit her, feeling an open, sticky gash. The wound was deep and long, but it didn't feel as though it had crushed bone.

Even still, if she didn't get it sewn soon, infection would set in, especially laying on this ship filled with death and disease.

Footsteps sounded above her.

"Please," she whispered, tears coming to her eyes. "Please, help me."

She whispered to God, to the devil, to the nymphs of the sea, anyone who was willing to listen, to offer her a way out.

The footsteps overhead moved closer, down a set of stairs and to just outside the door.

Guinevere closed her eyes, feigning sleep, but didn't bother to put the wool back on. Anyone looking in on her would see the puddle of vomit on the floor and know she'd woken at some point. Hopefully, they would just believe she'd fallen back asleep.

Light filtered from behind her eyes. Whoever was there had a lantern.

"You've woken." 'Twas General Gray.

She didn't answer. Didn't move. Kept her eyes closed. Fingers relaxed. Breathing even.

The light drew nearer, his footsteps echoing on the wood planks and then muffled by a thin rug.

The sound of the lantern being set down reached her a second before the bed shifted with his weight.

Cold fingers touched the side of her face, sliding over her cheek toward her lips where he dragged her lower lip down, the tip of his finger touching her teeth. It took every ounce of her willpower not to move, to gag. To scream at the top of her lungs and never stop.

Gray sucked in a ragged breath, that made her heart speed up and bile rise once more in her throat.

He was going to rape her. Of that, she was certain. When, was the question.

Lower, he moved, his hand sliding over her throat, pausing at her pulse point.

"You can keep your eyes closed if you want, but I know you're awake. Your heart is racing. Is it excitement? Fear? Perhaps a bit of both?"

She felt his weight press closer, leaning over her, breathing on her face. His lips touched her neck, pressing against her pulse, and Guinevere had to bite her tongue and swallow hard to keep from vomiting. The metallic taste of blood slid over her tongue—she'd bitten it that hard.

Gray's hands roamed over her chest, squeezing her breasts which were unprotected by a bodice in her thin nightrail. Her stomach rolled and she pulled her knees up, trying to roll away from him. He shoved her back flat.

"You're gorgeous."

She did not save her virginity for this man. As tired as she was, when he tried, she would force herself to fight, even if it meant passing out from the vigor of her blows.

He touched her thighs and she squeezed them shut, tight, but he pried them open despite her slapping at his face. He cupped her sex, his breathing going labored. She raked her nails over his cheek.

"Nay! Nay!" she screamed. Her eyes flew open, taking in his perverted expression. "Get. Off. Me." Her words sounded weak, quiet, but she'd said them all the same.

But he only laughed, blood from her scratches trickling down his face.

Chapter Nineteen

Unaware of how many English were on the lit ship, Brody and two dozen of the guards left Dunnottar, crowding into three rowboats and made their way toward the vessel.

They were quiet as they could be, dipping oars into the water and slowly pushing back, but with enough force to create a good momentum. When they reached the ship, Brody left first onto the rope ladder, climbing to the rails in record speed. Peering over the side, he scanned the empty deck. Whoever was aboard was below.

Cautiously, he stepped onto the surface and took off his boots, motioning for every man to do the same as they climbed over the rail, so their footsteps would be quieted.

In a whisper, he gave his orders. "Six of ye to every level. Three to each set of stairs at the bow and stern. I'll start with the officer's quarters. Leave no room, crate or corner unturned. Any English ye find—kill them. At all costs, protect my wife."

The men nodded and chose their levels. They then split up between the stairs.

Brody walked across the deck toward the stairs that led separately into the officer's quarters, his claymore drawn and gripped with both hands, prepared to slice off the head of any enemy he encountered. True to their talent, he could not hear his men as they traversed the ship. But what he could hear was his wife's voice, "Get. Off. Me." Followed by evil male laughter.

It could be none other than Gray!

Bastard!

A sudden surge of rage propelled Brody forward. He was blind with it. Going straight for the open doorway of the captain's cabin, he burst through.

Gray had Guinevere pinned to the bed, her nightrail raised up around her hips as he fumbled with his breeches. She fought valiantly against him, punching, kicking, scratching, biting.

Thank God she was alive. Blood soaked her hair, and even from here he could see the wound was deep.

Blind rage made it hard for him to find his voice, but when he did, he bellowed, "Get your bloody hands off my wife!"

Guinevere turned shocked eyes toward him, her pale face drawn. Tears stained her cheeks. And then recognition followed by relief.

213

Gray laughed and leapt from the bed. "I see you've arrived just in time to witness me taking your wife over and over and over again."

Brody bared his teeth. "You'll never take my wife."

Gray grinned and pulled his sword from his sheath, twirling it with the arrogance of a man who'd not yet lost a fight. "Oh, but there you're wrong, savage. She's already mine."

And how could he lose a fight when he preyed on those who might never have a chance to win?

Brody glanced at his wife who had curled up in a ball on the corner of the bed, her nightrail tucked over her ankles, knees into her chest. Her entire body trembled. She shook her head and mouthed, "Thank you."

Och, how it broke his heart. She needn't thank him. He would have come for her any day, any time. No matter the enemy. No matter the cost. He'd made a vow and he meant to honor it.

Brody swallowed the burn in his throat. He kept his gaze level on the man he'd been waiting months to thrust his sword through. "I know who ye are." Brody gripped his sword tighter, taking two slow steps forward. "I know the sins ye've committed. And I know just when ye're going to die."

"Do tell." Gray sneered and raised his own sword, half the size of Brody's.

"General Gray. Enemy of the Scots. Raper of women. Murderer of men. Ye'll not live beyond the next few minutes."

"Funny how a dead man could get things so right and yet so wrong." Gray arched his sword bringing it down toward Brody in a violent attack.

Brody easily blocked the blow. "Ye'll burn forever in hell for your sins, raped a thousand and one times by the devil himself, and then for eternity by his demons."

Gray laughed, a slow, malevolent sound. "I know who you are, savage. Marischal Keith, heir to the barbarian I killed. Brother to sweet, sweet Johanna." The man made a vulgar motion with his tongue and then grabbed at the crotch of his breeches.

Brody could no longer think beyond feeling the bastard's blood on his hands. He attacked, his sword cutting the air enough to make it sing as he brought it sideways toward Gray's ribs. The general leapt, blocking at the last second and faltering.

"She screamed and screamed," the bastard said. "Crying out 'help'. But no one would come. And I took her. Oh, how I took her again and again. Just like I will do with your sweet Guinevere."

Rage filled Brody, and all he could do was hack and hack at his enemy. Gray fought him off, but he wasn't filled with as much wrath as Brody. And the taunts he tossed only fueled the anger and viciousness of Brody's attack. He sliced into the general's right arm, cutting deep, and watching the blood pour.

Gray cried out dropping his sword. But Brody didn't want it to be over that quickly.

"Pick it up," he growled.

Gray lifted his weapon with his right hand, true worry creasing his face for the first time.

"At last, ye see the brevity of your life. Who is the dead man now?" Brody toyed with the man some more, slicing into his legs, his shoulders, his back, his cheeks. Cutting deep, slicing shallow. He wanted the man to suffer. To feel the pain that every one of his victims had felt before they died. He cut off his ears, the tip of his nose. Hacked at his hair. His fingers. Stabbed into his feet. Cut straight through his groin.

With blood dripping from his sliced lips, General Gray dropped to his knees, his sword falling and he held out his arms. "End me."

Brody shook his head. "Nay."

"End me!" Gray bellowed.

"Ye will burn. Ye will feel it."

Brody wiped his sword on the rotted blanket covering the bed and lifted his wife into his arms, cradling her. He kissed her brow and murmured how brave she was, that he would take her home, keep her safe. She was cold and trembling, her teeth chattering.

General Gray started to crawl for the door, but Brody wasn't about to let him escape, only to drown, and make a quick death of himself. Brody knocked the lantern to the floor, fire igniting on the decaying floorboards, the dry-rotted rug.

He stood there for a moment, arms around Guinevere, watching as the flames licked closer and closer to Gray as he backed away from the blaze until he was trapped in the corner of the room.

Only then did Brody leave, satisfied he'd avenged his loved ones—all of them.

"Abandon ship!" Brody bellowed, rushing up the stairs to the main deck.

He charged the warning bell, ringing it ferociously. His men appeared from the stairs, running to the rails.

"Take her," he said, trying to thrust Guinevere toward one of his men so he could make certain she was safely off the ship as he determined that all of his men were safe as well.

"Nay! Don't let me go," she cried out, clinging to his neck and burying her face in his shoulder. "Don't," she sobbed.

Brody didn't have the heart to force her. She'd already been through so much. He held her tight to him and nodded for his men to disembark. Each of them gave a report that there were no other men alive on the ship. The only men they'd encountered were the flesh and bones of the dead from smallpox outbreak months before.

Gray's screams surrounded them as he burned, and the creaking sounds the ship was making warned him of its imminent collapse.

"Can ye climb?" he asked Guinevere.

"I... I don't know."

"I'll carry ye." Brody set her down just before the rail and climbed over. "Come here." He helped her to lift her leg, until she was over the rail. "Wrap your arms and legs around me."

She gave a slight nod, reaching for him, her cold limbs circling his. He kept one arm firmly around her waist, the other holding onto the rope ladder as he descended. Guinevere tucked her head against his shoulder, clinging to him.

"How did you get here so fast?" she murmured. "I was just praying for help and then you appeared. 'Tis the second time you've saved me. Are you my guardian angel?"

Brody chuckled softly and pressed his lips to her cheek. "I'll be whatever ye want me to be, *iasg beag.*"

"I want you to be my husband."

"I am."

"Nay, in truth."

"I promised we'd wed before God as soon as the kirk was built. I still promise it."

She nodded. "I've no reason to doubt you."

"And I hope to never give ye one."

They reached the rowboat and his men helped them to settle. Guinevere still clung to him, but her eyes were closed, and he prayed she'd not yet succumbed to her wound. He bent low to listen to her breath against his ear and ordered his men to row as though a gale storm was upon them. Behind them, the blazing ship thundered as floor after floor collapsed and the masts fell one by one, splintering the rails. Once on shore, Brody lifted her in his arms and ran up the one hundred sixty stairs, hollering for a healer.

A look behind him at the sea showed only a tiny flame sizzling out as the ship sunk to the bottom.

Brody carried his wife up to her chamber, settling her on the bed.

Noah and her maid, Elinor, rushed in, the other woman looking just as beaten as his wife. Dear God, what had these women been through?

The healer came, clucking over Guinevere and issuing orders. When she tried to push Brody away, he nearly tossed the old crone out of the window until she asked him if he wanted her to help his wife or not. She cleaned the wound, cutting the hair close to the scalp so she could see it better. When his wife woke, screaming and flailing, he soothed her with calm words and gave her sips of an herbal draught the healer brewed until she once more fell asleep and the healer could work.

"She'll not be pleased with the state of her hair," the healer murmured when she was done.

"She will be grateful," Brody said, having no doubt. "My wife is kind."

"Aye." The healer met his gaze. "She is a good woman. Ye're lucky to have her."

Brody nodded, his chest swelling. To have a Scot tell him he was lucky to have his English wife meant a lot to him. She'd made an impression on the people here. And he was proud of her.

"I'll be seeing to her maid now." The healer took Elinor into her own chamber, shutting the door behind them.

Noah looked antsy, shuffling his feet by the door, and fiddling with the dagger at his hip.

"What is it?"

"I…" He glanced toward the closed adjoining door.

"Ye wish to be with the lady's maid?"

Noah pursed his lips, then nodded. "Aye."

"Ye dinna need my permission to stand by her side. But afore ye do, tell me what happened to the English army and where did ye find the maid?"

"We fought them. Without their leader, they were unorganized, half-hearted. Those who did not engage ran, and we let them. They won't last long." Noah flicked his gaze to Guinevere's sleeping form. "Lady Elinor was in the dungeon, already rats had bitten at her toes. She was terrified, didn't let go of my hand until just now when the healer took her."

"Saints. Have they figured out who's betrayed me? Who allowed Gray in?"

"The lad, Toby, he broke down and confessed to helping take the ladies. To paying off the guard at the postern to open the gate. I tossed him where we found Lady Elinor and he's named a few others." Noah edged toward the door, but Brody could tell he was hiding something.

"Is that all?"

Noah paused and blew out a long breath. "Nay."

"Tell me."

"I'd hoped to avoid telling ye just yet… Mrs. Donald was behind it. Toby says she convinced him all the English should die on account of what happened to Johanna and your father. That they were to rid the castle of vermin, that they were doing it for ye."

"Bloody hell, she willingly gave my wife over to the verra man who committed those heinous crimes." Brody was torn between needing to stay at his wife's side and needing to find Mrs. Donald to punish her.

"Aye."

"Where is she?"

"They're still searching for her, my laird. They will find her. Have no doubt. She'll find no safe passage among the people. They love your wife too much."

"And the guards who betrayed me?"

"They are in the dungeon with Toby. They claimed not to have realized that she was going to Gray, but that they thought she would be put on the ship to sail back to England with her father, that Lord Arundel had come to claim her. That ye had requested it be so."

"Rubbish! They lie!"

"Aye."

"I will see them all whipped and hanged for their crimes."

Noah continued to edge toward the door.

"Go." Brody raised a brow. "But dinna forget your alliance to Chief Oliphant's daughter."

"I know well my duty," he grumbled.

The door closed and Brody turned his attention back to his sleeping wife.

"I never thought I'd be here," Brody whispered to her. "With ye. With any woman that I... cared for." He touched her forehead, so pale. "Heal, wife. Heal for the both of us."

"Brody..." Guinevere whispered.

"Sleep, *iasg beag*."

"I'm no fish..." Her voice was faint, but he clearly heard the words.

Even in a drug-induced sleep she argued with him. Brody smiled, for it was a sign that she was already well on her way to getting better.

Chapter Twenty

Guinevere's eyes flew open, her arms jerked, prepared to fend off Gray and his deplorable touch.

But she was no longer on the ship.

She blinked rapidly, certain she was dreaming, as her own chamber came into view. Familiar tapestries hung from the wall, the curtains of her bed were halfway open, and sitting in a high-back chair beside her was Brody, fast asleep.

Dunnottar. And it was real. This was in her chamber. She pinched herself just to be sure.

But how had she gotten here?

Then she remembered, Gray had been on top of her and Brody had burst through the captain's door. Looming there resembling a dragon. A fierce fight had ensued, she'd never seen the likes of before. Her husband had saved her. She remembered only a few fleeting moments after, him carrying her. A fire. But then her memory went black. She must have finally succumbed to her injury.

And now she was back here.

Raising her fingers, she felt a bandage wrapped around her head, covering the wound.

Her head no longer pounded from the spot, simply a very dull ache, but her body... She felt so heavy. Thirsty. Incredibly starving.

Sensing her consciousness, Brody jolted awake, leaning forward, touching her arm. She met his gaze and tried to smile. "Hello."

He grinned. "Good morning," he whispered.

Saints but she could have stared at him all day. Handsome as ever, his eyes were filled with emotion, his jaw covered in a fine layer of stubble. "I slept through the night, husband. I'm starving."

"Ye've slept through many a night, and I suspect the broth we've been feeding ye doesn't last long in the belly." He touched her forehead. "Your fever has broken."

"Fever?"

"Aye. Ye've had a fever a little over a week." Worry lines creased the corners of his eyes. "I'm glad 'tis over."

She licked her lips and before she could ask, he brought a cup to her mouth.

"Drink."

She sipped slowly, the cool ale blissful on her tongue.

"I'll ring for a proper meal." Brody stood, but then bent over her, kissing her forehead. "So many will be pleased ye've woken. I'll send for the healer, as well. She'll want to take a look at ye."

"Wait." Guinevere grabbed hold of his hand, noting how much larger he was than her, how strong.

"Aye, sweetheart." He sat on the edge of the bed beside her, a comforting weight.

"Before I see anyone…" She glanced around the room. "I need to know something." She licked her lips and reached for the cup. Who knew talking could drain her so much and make her mouth so much drier?

And Brody, patient as a saint, helped her.

"What happened?" she asked. "Where is Gray? Elinor? Mrs. Donald?" Her gaze darted for the door and then back to her cup, fearing the woman was still undiscovered and that poison lay in the ale.

Guinevere shuddered. The hatred that had spilled from their cook was still tangible, thick, filling the room.

"Gray is dead, love. Elinor is safe, I believe out for a walk now with Noah, and Mrs. Donald awaits ye in the dungeon."

"The dungeon." She imagined the woman brooding as she rotted however many days it had been.

"Aye."

"And her accomplices?"

"I believe we got them all. And when ye're ready, ye can take a look and tell me if we did."

Guinevere shook her head. "I only saw Mrs. Donald and Toby. They covered my head. I know there was a guard or two at the gate, but that's it. And then Gray…" She shivered, feeling the pain of her ordeal all over again. "No one here likes me, Brody. They all want me to leave." And some wanted her to die.

Brody gripped her hand and pulled it to is lips, brushing her knuckles. "Nay, that isn't true. I like ye."

She couldn't help but smile. "I'm not certain that's enough."

His gaze turned serious. "Ye'll be surprised to find that there are many who do. Many who have expressed their concern, brought ye gifts."

"Many?" She raised a skeptical brow. Nay, she didn't believe it.

"Aye. Look." He swept his arm toward the table where she ate some of her meals to see several packages.

"Scottish?" Her tone was incredulous. "But..."

"Dinna fash over it now." Brody brushed the hair away from her face, lovingly. "Let us get ye well and then we can sort it all out."

Guinevere gazed around the room, peering into the shadows. She tucked. She held tight to Brody's hand. "I am afraid."

"I haven't let ye out of my sight since I found ye, love. Slept right here in this chair. When I needed to use the privy, Noah stayed with ye, or Elinor. I willna let anyone harm ye again, and trust me, all that reside within these walls and the surrounding village feel the same."

Guinevere nodded, but she didn't feel confident in his words. What would happen the next time he left? Would someone try to abduct her again?

She could still feel Gray's hands on her. See the hatred curling Mrs. Donald's lips.

Brody kissed her hand again and she found herself wishing he'd kiss her lips, to feel the comfort of his embrace. To wash away the touch of Gray.

"Can ye ever forgive me?" he asked.

"You did your duty, husband. I cannot fault you for serving your king. And I cannot fault you for the evil minds of others. There is nothing to forgive."

"But if I'd not left, ye would not have been hurt."

"There is no telling whether or not that is true. Mrs. Donald… She disliked me from the very start. She fed me slop meant for the pigs, tricked me into thinking it was you who demanded I fix the door. She said awful, cruel things to me. Told me you wished me to stay in my chamber all day long. Her hatred, it ate away at her. I do not think your being here or gone would have stopped her eventual attempt to get rid of me. To be rid of any English in the castle. In her own twisted way, she sought to protect you." Guinevere avoided his gaze. "To avenge your family." Brody had not told her about his past, or at least he'd not had the chance to yet, and she felt ugly for the way she'd found out.

"There is no excuse for what she did. Ye canna harm one innocent in order to avenge another."

"I forgive her."

"What?" Brody looked shocked.

"She hurt me, aye, but I am still here. She did not win. I pity her." And that was the truth. If someone could be filled that much with hate, then how could she add more hate on top of that? Hate could only be combatted with love.

"Ye're a good woman, Guinevere. A kind soul ye have, but ye're brave and fierce, too. I'm proud to call ye my wife."

His words warmed her heart, made her chest swell with pride.

"I should have told ye... about Johanna, and my father. Perhaps if I had—" He cut himself off abruptly, sorrow filling his eyes.

"Sharing your demons with me would not have protected me, Brody. You are a fierce warrior, a great leader, loyal to your future king. There is no doubt in that. And your family, they know that. I'm certain that others have told you that you cannot blame yourself for what happened, because it's true, and I know that doesn't matter to you. That you do blame yourself. That you search for ways in which you could have predicted what happened and defended them. I only hope that, one day, you can forgive yourself, as I'm certain that is what they would wish. I am sorry for what happened to your sister, your father. And I wish I could take away your pain. Gray was an evil man and I hope that his death has helped to heal you some."

"I was terrified the same fate was in store for ye," Brody whispered. "I went mad with rage, with worry. I think part of the reason I went after ye on the beach, before we were wed, was because I saw Johanna in ye. I thought if I could simply save this one lass and her maids..."

"And ye did. Twice. Gray, he did not..." She waved her hands, unable to put her voice to such an ugly word.

"I know, love."

"I..." She glanced away, certain that now was not quite the time to tell him she was still a virgin. Instead, she smiled and squeezed his hand. "Will you help me sit up?"

"Aye." Brody stood beside her, lifting her into a seated position and fitting her pillows behind her back until she was comfortable.

She closed her eyes, for a moment feeling dizzy, but it quickly passed.

"I should get your meal," he murmured.

"Not yet. I still want a few minutes to just be… with you. Will you hold me a minute?"

"Ye need only ask." He climbed onto the bed beside her, tucking her against him.

She rested her head on his shoulder feeling so much safer with him there.

They lay still for a little while, quiet and thoughtful, sliding their fingers together, entwining and untwining them. It felt so natural, this quietness. Touching. As though they'd always done so.

Brody broke the silence. "There is something else."

She glanced up at him, taking in the worried expression creasing his brow. Brody's grip on her hand tightened just a bit as though he were afraid she'd leap from the bed and run away.

"Tell me, Brody."

"Your father… He is here."

"Oh." She breathed out, until her lungs felt ready to collapse. "And, ye haven't murdered each other yet?"

Brody chuckled. "We've gotten fairly close."

"I would speak to him."

"He has come to visit ye each day."

"He's not in your dungeon is he?"

He stroked her cheek. "Nay, *iasg beag*. He's got a chamber."

"Is he overly furious?"

"Nay. He is remorseful, but I shall let him explain that later. For now, let me call for a meal."

"I *am* famished."

Another week passed with the healer insisting that she stay in bed. Guinevere was going mad with the need to be outside, but Brody kept her plenty entertained, reading to her from his own journal in which he'd documented his days at war. Brody was a good writer, and regaled her with stories of the enemy, tournaments and caber tossing. They cried together when he relayed the Battle of Dunbar, which ended in the fate of his sister and father, and then made plans to bring his mother and sister, Maire, to Dunnottar for their wedding celebration. When he wasn't reading to her, Brody taught her how to play knucklebones, which she excelled at and when she'd cleaned his pouch of coin, he brought her a chess board with pieces he'd carved himself.

She let him win the first three games before she decided to teach him a lesson in strategy.

Between games, while they ate, they told each other stories of their childhoods, shared their dreams, their fears, and their wishes.

Brody left her alone only to take care of his personal business, returning smelling fresh and delicious. Elinor came each morning to help her do the same, braiding her hair, just below the bandage.

Guinevere and Brody held hands, unconsciously, most of the time, and sometimes, consciously, she would reach for him. When her father came to see her, Brody tried to excuse himself, but she asked him to stay.

Her father blubbered into his hands begging her forgiveness, that he'd not known Gray's intent or he never would have sent the man her way. That he should have seen the man's vile nature from the beginning but he'd been blind to it like a fool.

Guinevere forgave her father, telling him that though she was fine, there were warning signs of the general's personality and, in hindsight, she should have told him.

But her father, and Brody, both protested that she was to take none of the blame onto her own shoulders.

She fully expected her father to leave then, to travel back to England, but then he sprung on her some news she'd not expected. After long conversations with Brody, he'd sent for her mother and sisters. They would soon be living at one of Brody's holdings in the north—he'd joined the Scottish rebellion. After realizing that there were so many men like Gray, that even his own king was like the general, he wanted nothing to do with them.

It was shocking to say the least, but she confessed that she, too, had felt the change over the last year.

Just shy of three weeks after her injury, the stitches long since removed and the hair that had been cut short growing back—neatly hidden by a plait Elinor had designed that wound around her head like a cap—the healer gave permission for Guinevere to leave her chamber.

She descended to the great hall amid cheers from the servants and clansmen and women present for the trial of Mrs. Donald, Toby and their accomplices.

"Ye're prepared?" Brody whispered.

She squeezed his arm where she held him and he patted her hand. "It has been too long. We must decide their fate. They've languished long enough."

"As ye wish, my dear." Brody led her toward the two high-backed chairs in the center of the great hall.

The trestle tables had been pushed up against the walls, benches tucked underneath, and people filled the space. The great hall had been transformed from a place of feasting to a place of judgment.

Once she was settled in her chair, Brody called the people to attention.

"Today, we come here to judge and sentence those who betrayed me. Who injured my wife and put her life in danger. Your mistress, Lady Guinevere, is a part of me, a part of this clan, a part of this castle, a part of Scotland. What is done to her, is done to me. All those who oppose this, leave now, and never return. All those in allegiance, kneel."

The room lowered at once, every man, woman and child, regardless of age, bent to their knees, hands over their hearts and shouted their allegiance.

"Bring in the accused." Brody nodded to Noah who left by a side door and returned a moment later with six people in chains, led by guards.

"The men and women before ye stand accused of treason. Abduction. Assault."

Brody met the eyes of the six before them but Guinevere found it a little more difficult.

She dragged in a deep breath, prepared to face head on those who wanted her dead, were willing to risk their own lives to see it done. And when she did, all she felt was pity. No hatred. No anger.

"All have confessed to their crimes. Crimes punishable by death." Brody let those words hang in the air.

The six, Mrs. Donald, Toby, another kitchen maid, and three guards, hung their heads in shame, already resigned to their fate, having lain in the dungeon for three weeks.

"But, your mistress, Lady Guinevere, has asked that I show mercy. No one will die today by our hands. The women are to receive twenty lashes. The men fifty. And all of ye are banished from Keith lands."

Gasps went up through the crowd, and while five muttered their gratitude with slack jaws and vacant eyes, one fiery, hatred-filled glare centered on Guinevere.

Mrs. Donald.

The woman spoke not a word, but her gaze said enough.

Guinevere held her enemy's stare, strengthening with each moment that passed. She stood and walked toward the prisoners, her gaze never wavering from their cook.

"When I showed you kindness, you showed me naught. When I showed you good will, you showed me naught. And now, when I show you mercy, you show me hate. But know this"—she pressed her hand to her heart—"I forgive you. I forgive you the evil that lies in your heart, the vileness that licks at your thoughts. For the rest of my days, I will endeavor to forget you. But I know you, you will never forget that somewhere in Scotland is a lady who gave you your life."

CHAPTER TWENTY-ONE

Ordinarily, after an emotional and challenging ordeal, Guinevere felt completely exhausted. But not so this time around.

After the prisoners were escorted off of Keith lands, Guinevere spent the better part of two hours greeting and listening to the people of Dunnottar. They were kind, generous, and wanted to make it known to her that they loved her, respected her, wanted her as their mistress. That they were grateful for all the things she'd done. Before de Ros had taken the castle, the monks had led peaceful lives and done good works much like what she did, and they were so pleased that she'd embodied that.

They felt cherished, and in turn, wanted her to feel the same way.

Brody waved her over and whispered, "I had our supper served in your chamber."

"Oh, thank you." He knew her so well. He knew she would soon be exhausted, or at least need the solitude of a moment's peace. "And it is *our* chamber. You have slept there every night since returning."

His eyes widened slightly. "This is true. How is your head?" he asked.

"Much better. The tincture the healer gave me keeps the pain at bay, but leaves my mind clear."

"I am pleased to hear it." He offered her his arm and she took it.

Together, they bid good night to the people.

She spied Elinor near the hearth, deeply engrossed in a conversation with Noah. They leaned close together, happiness shining in both of their eyes. Seeing it lifted Guinevere's heart as much as it saddened her.

"I fear she's falling in love with your cousin," Guinevere said.

Brody glanced toward the hearth, knowing instantly of whom she spoke. They'd had similar conversations often.

"I hope he doesn't break her heart."

"Or the other way around. But it seems inevitable that they will both be hurt by the bond they've formed, given he's promised to another." Guinevere chuckled. "And there is also that Elinor has long maintained she seeks the company of more than one man for the rest of her days.

Brody chuckled. "And ye, my dear wife? What about ye?"

Guinevere glanced at Brody out of the side of her eyes. This was a topic she'd tried to broach more than once, but had not yet done so.

They'd been married for two months now, and Brody had not asked to bed her. Granted, he'd not initially had the chance, but she'd given him several hints over the last week when she was feeling better, when he was lying beside her in bed, but still he hesitated.

"It is my sincerest hope to share my bed with only one man my whole life."

Brody's smile faltered and she knew he would assume she referred to de Ros.

"There is something I must tell you," she whispered, feeling her face heat as they exited the hall.

"Tell me," Brody said, stopping at the foot of the stairs.

Guinevere touched his shirt, twirling her fingers around the ties. "I have never... I am..." Her voice was so shaky, as were her hands.

She'd shared so much with Brody over the past few weeks, and yet this one part of her, she'd not been able to divulge, though not for lack of trying.

"I dinna care if ye canna have children," he said softly. "Noah has always been my heir and he can remain so."

Guinevere let out a nervous laugh at his assumption, continuing to keep her gaze focused on his shirt ties. "'Tis not that. I wouldn't know besides."

Brody frowned and then lifted her chin with his fingers, so that she had to look him in the eye. "Say it plainly, love."

Guinevere sucked in a deep breath, then blurted out, "I am still a virgin."

Brody looked taken aback. "How is that possible?"

She shrugged. "De Ros... He and I never... He never could."

"Ah." Brody nodded, understanding even though she'd barely uttered anything intelligible. "I can. And I will. When the time comes."

"I think that time has come."

"Och... lass..." His eyes darkened and he lifted her in his arms, carrying her the rest of the way up the stairs. He burst through their chamber door, barring it behind them. Set out on the table was a small feast, the fire in the hearth was blazing and several candles were lit around the room.

Guinevere giggled at his speed to get to their room, feeling light, happy, excited. With her arms around his neck, she leaned her head against his shoulder and whispered, "I didn't think happiness could be mine."

"Before I met ye, I was certain it was a fantasy." Brody carried her toward her bed. "Ye have changed me, lass. I dinna know how, but ye have."

They reached the edge of the bed and he started to lower her, then stopped. His lips were only a breath from hers, his eyelids low. A heady sensation filled her.

"I know I promised I'd wait three months..." he murmured. "And I will maintain that promise if ye wish it."

Guinevere shook her head, dragging her fingers through his hair. "I don't want to wait."

"I want to make love to ye, wife." His mouth edged closer to hers.

"Aye." She closed her eyes, anticipating the delicious touch of his lips.

And then warm velvet caressed her mouth. His kiss was tender, enticing. He brushed his lips back and forth over hers. Gentle. Soft. Not invasive. Tantalizing.

When she leaned into his kiss, growing bolder, he licked teasingly and then nibbled on her lower lip. Guinevere's entire body came alive. She tugged his hair, opening her mouth for further exploration. Oh! The touch of his tongue on hers... Would that she could kiss him like this forever. She felt like she was swirling up in a fluffy white cloud of pleasure. The way he touched her, oh, but she was melting...boneless.

"My wife," Brody murmured, laying her on the bed. "Mine. Forever."

If he only knew how much his words lifted her—and overwhelmed her. Guinevere clung to him, tugging him down over her.

He touched her face, stroking, gentle, all while his mouth made love to hers. The way he kissed her, touched her, she felt cherished, warm and... even loved. This was the way it was supposed to be between a man and a woman. Pleasure and heat and desire all wrapped up in a cocoon of emotion.

"I..." She bit her tongue, about to tell him that she loved him. How had it happened? So fast? It struck her like lightning making her heart soar.

Brody pressed his hands to either side of her face, his gaze locked on hers. "*Tha gaol agam ort, iasg beag.*"

"What does that mean?" she whispered, recognizing his endearment for her. At first she'd hated him calling her little fish, but the nickname had grown on her and she found it comforting and sweet now.

"I will tell ye later." And then his lips were on her. Passionate. All consuming.

And it hit her then, as much as she wanted it, that they could be happy together, that their marriage would be one filled with love. Her heart warmed. Oh, how Guinevere wanted him. There was no turning back now. She would forge ahead, just like a warrior did in battle. Brody, Scotland, they were her present and her future.

Guinevere held tight to him, returning his searing kiss. She gave him all she was in that kiss. Stroked her tongue over his, tasting the sweet apple he'd eaten in the great hall.

Brody groaned, exploring her shoulders, her breasts, caressing gently over her nipples. At first she was nervous at his touch, but within seconds, she had pushed away her trepidations and put herself fully at his delicious mercy. Thank goodness she did, because his touch was pure wonderment.

She trailed her fingers over the muscled length of his arms and back, reveling in the corded sinew as he flexed and relaxed beneath her caress.

Brody slid his mouth from her lips to her chin, down the column of her neck. Every slide of his tongue sent chills racing along her limbs. She whimpered as he skimmed up to her ear, sucked gently on an earlobe.

"Ye are so beautiful, Guinevere," he whispered against her ear. "I want to please ye. I want to make ye sing with joy."

His words had her heart turning over in response and she felt like she could fly. Brody pulled away for a moment, gazing down at her, his nose sliding over hers in affection.

"You already are," she whispered. "Do I please you?"

He trailed his fingertips over her heart, brushing the milky tops of her breasts. She sucked in a quickened breath.

"Aye, love." His voice was husky with desire, sending frissons of pleasure along her spine.

"Kiss me..." She leaned up toward him, capturing his lips with her own, and melting once more into his heated embrace.

Brody kissed her until she had no breath left, but he didn't relent in his pursuit of her pleasure. He dipped his head to her neck, trailing his lips to the valley between her breasts.

"Ye've too much clothes on." He tugged lightly on her gown until her hardened nipple was exposed. He captured the tip between his teeth, teasing gently.

The gentle tug of his teeth and heat of his breath had her moaning and arching her back. She dug her fingers into the muscles of his back. "Then undress me."

The tingling in the pit of her stomach built, filling her core with need. Between her thighs delicious sensations washed over her, leaving a slickness in its wake.

"Dear heavens, I've been wanting to do that for months." Brody climbed from the bed and pulled her to stand with him.

Brody unlaced her gown and slowly slid it up over her waist, her breasts, taking the time to kiss her belly, her ribs. She shivered but not from cold, from pleasure and need. Delicious, hot need.

He slid the fabric over her head and along her arms, kissing the dip of each elbow. When that was done, he removed her chemise, tossing both items to the floor.

Emboldened by his quick skill at seeing her nude, she trailed her fingers down his chest and hooked them into the belt of his plaid, skimming the flesh of his waist. He was warm, soft and yet so hard.

"Och, lass, ye are driving me to madness…"

He undressed quickly, and she watched, unable to look away. She realized then, she'd never even seen him without a shirt, let alone nude. She wasn't shy as she examined him. His muscled chest, long, strong legs. Flat, contoured belly. A sprinkle of dark hair covered his chest, leading to a straight line that went all the way to his… Shaft. Thick and hard with need, she blanched. Lord, but he was well-endowed.

Brody didn't give her more time to contemplate his body. His body collided with hers and he walked her backward toward the bed until her knees hit the edge and she lay back. He followed her, sliding her up the length of the mattress and nudging her thighs gently apart, where he settled. She jumped at the contact of his hard shaft pressed so hotly against her. Brody groaned, his forehead falling to hers, and he captured her lips again for a thoroughly arousing kiss.

Wrapping her arms around his neck, she dredged her fingers through his hair. "Oh, Brody," she whispered into his kiss.

"*Mo chridhe, mo chridhe.*"

He growled, dragging his lips from hers to travel down her neck and over her breasts. His mouth was hot velvet, driving her to the brink of madness. She writhed beneath him, arched her back and then writhed some more when that move brought increased contact of his hardness to her sex.

He took her mouth back in a hungry kiss and she met his tongue thrust for thrust, feeding her own hunger. She instinctively spread her thighs wide, her knees bending upward to hug his hips. Without Brody, she never would have realized that making love could be so amazing. Blood pounded a hypnotic rhythm through her veins. Every part of her trembled with yearning, with a need for more. She couldn't believe this was happening and that she was enjoying every moment of it. Savoring it. Passion overwhelmed her.

Magnus swept his hands from each of her ankles up her thighs, leaving shivers in his wake. He leaned up on his elbows and gazed into her eyes.

His face was a storm cloud of desire and intensity.

"I want ye, iasg beag. Are ye afraid?" His fingers brushed feather-like over her belly.

Guinevere sucked in her breath, enjoying the delicious tendrils that wrapped around her, settling in her core. "I'm not. I want you, too."

"Good." His grin was full of promise and he leaned in to kiss the spot just below her ear

"Oh…" She was lost in pleasure.

He kissed her again, lingeringly, lazily, but she deepened the kiss, not wanting it to be slow. A craving like she'd never known filled her. Heating her blood.

Guinevere spread her legs a little wider, liking how his hard member settled against the cleft of her thighs. She lifted her hips, trying to get a little closer.

"Och, lass, if ye keep that up, 'twill be over before it begins."

She grinned, happy to know she could have just as much effect on Brody as he had on her. "I like it," she answered.

"Oh, I like it, too," he said, his voice strangled.

He reached his fingers between their bodies. She bucked her hips as his thumb brushed over the sensitive nub there.

"Ye are so wet already," he murmured, his finger sliding inside her.

Her entire body felt alive with heady, enchanting pleasure. She was drowning in it. A delicious pressure built within her, radiating from her core and down her thighs. She spread her legs wider, rocked her hips in time with the strokes of Brody's fingers inside her, over her, around her, everywhere.

She gasped for breath, certain she was about to ignite.

And then she did. An explosion of fiery sensations burst throughout her body. She cried out, clutching her husband's shoulders as the waves took over.

"*Mo chreach*," he growled against her ear before he kissed her savagely.

She kissed him back with as much intensity as she could muster, greedily accepting whatever pleasure he would give her.

He probed her core once more. "Ye're ready for me." He notched his erection at her entrance and her stomach did a little nervous flip.

This time his entry was not as pleasant. He surged forward, breaking the barrier of her virginity with his thick shaft. She cried out again, only this time in pain. Brody sank all the way inside her, stretching her uncomfortably. What a great lie! All this pleasure only to end in pain. She pushed against him, wriggled her hips in an effort to get away from him.

"Shh...love. Dinna move. The pain, 'twill only last a minute."

And he was right. Brody nibbled at her lips, whispered soft words of encouragement, talked of her beauty, of his desire for her. He kissed her neck, dipped his head lower to tease her breasts. The pain dissipated and once again she found herself writhing beneath him, his invasion a bewildering welcome. The delicious pleasure she'd felt before returned, tenfold.

"Better?" he murmured.

"Aye." She opened her eyes to see him gazing down at her, his lips wet from their kiss, his eyes full of concern. She felt such a surge of emotion then it nearly brought her to tears.

He smiled slowly, a wicked grin. "And this? How does this feel?" He slid slowly out of her and pushed gently back inside.

"Oh!" Decadent sensations vibrated from her center outward.

Brody gave an arrogant chuckle. "Indeed."

He claimed her mouth again, his tongue snaking inside to duel with hers, thrusting in time with his body. Guinevere wrapped her legs higher around his hips allowing him to thrust deeper, her pleasure intensifying.

Ecstasy took her breath, her mind. Her eyes widened, her nails dragged over Brody's shoulders and she arched her back while he thrust again and again. She cried out in release, the sensations strengthened by Brody's moans and quickened pace. He, too, cried out, his head thrown back as he drove briskly inside her, a great shudder rocking his entire body.

Brody collapsed to the side of her, tugging her against him, his breathing as rapid as her own.

"*Tha gaol agam ort, iasg beag*... I love ye, little fish."

Guinevere's mouth fell open and before she could respond, he kissed her with renewed passion.

Chapter Twenty-Two

"The first real snow has fallen."

Brody rolled to the side of the bed, having just woken, and saw his wife standing by the window, wrapped in a plaid, the smooth cream of one shoulder exposed, her bare feet curled against the wood floor.

She flashed him a smile, her eyes sparkling. "You're finally awake."

"Someone kept me up most of the night," he teased. Brody climbed from the bed and walked, naked, toward the window.

Guinevere opened her plaid blanket and he wrapped it around the both of them, as he stood behind her, his arms around her waist. He rested his chin on top of her head and gazed out at the tranquil landscape. Snow covered the ground in a sheet of sparkling white.

"Do ye like snow?" he asked.

Guinevere shrugged. "I've never thought about it. I hate to be cold."

"I want ye to try something. I made it as a lad."

"All right."

They dressed and he took her hand, leading her toward the kitchen where he grabbed two mugs. Outside, he filled the mugs with snow.

"What are you doing? Are you going to make me eat snow?" She giggled. "I've not eaten it since I was a wee thing."

"More than that." He winked.

Back in the kitchen, he asked their new cook, Matilda, if she minded if he used a few things. Of course, she didn't deny him, and even offered to help, but he declined.

"I want to teach my wife a treat. Something special we'll make for our children every winter."

Children. Guinevere's eyes widened at the same time his own did. Their gazes locked. They'd made love tenderly several times throughout the night. All through that time, not once had they discussed what the end result of their unions could be. Aye. Children. They would have them. Possibly, they'd already created one.

"Milk, vanilla, honey and cinnamon." He set the ingredients out on the cooking table and Guinevere tugged up a chair.

She appeared intrigued, and he liked the idea of teaching her something. Showing her a piece of himself, a tradition they could savor and share with their own children. Their family.

Lord, but he never thought he'd have one.

How different the world seemed now. All it had taken was the fiery temper of one English lass and his entire future had changed.

"Now, we're going to slowly pour in the milk," Brody said, showing her how he slowly poured the milk, stirring the snow at the same time. "We dinna want to melt the snow too much, that ruins the texture."

"Can I try?" Guinevere asked, reaching for a cup.

"Aye." He passed her the jug. "Just a touch."

Guinevere poured the milk like an expert.

"Are ye certain ye've not done this before?" he asked.

"Positive." She flashed a radiant smile.

Brody leaned down and kissed her, unable to help himself. "Now add in the honey and a dash of spices."

"Smells delicious." Her hand skimmed over his back.

"Aye." He kissed her brow. "And so do ye."

"What is it?" Matilda called from the corner of the kitchen where she was plucking a chicken.

Brody raised his eyes, having forgotten they were not alone. "I call it snow milk."

"Snow milk?" Matilda frowned. "Sounds unappetizing."

"'Tis delightful, I swear it," Brody laughed. He wiggled his brows at Guinevere and handed her a spoon. "Try it."

She dipped her spoon in the icy milk and pulled it to her lips, surprise and pleasure showing on her face. "Wow," she mused. "I am surprised, this is quite delicious."

Matilda sauntered over, examining the creamy frozen mixture.

"Try it," Brody encouraged.

She held up her hands, shaking them and backing away. "I couldna, my laird."

"Well, then make one yourself when we're not looking. 'Tis quite delicious. I promise."

Brody offered his wife his arm and they carried their snow milk to the great hall where they settled before the hearth to eat their frozen treat, toes near the heat.

"How did you ever discover such a thing?" Guinevere asked.

"Quite by accident." Brody chuckled at the memory. "I was a troublesome lad. My father was forever chasing me with a strap."

Guinevere raised her brow, a teasing smile curling her lips. "I want to hear the story of how you accidently discovered something so delectable."

"All right. I was skulking about the kitchens. Many guests had been stuck overnight from a feast, given it had snowed unexpectedly. Cook was preparing a honeyed milk for one of the ladies who had a stomach upset. But I wanted it for myself. I'd just swiped a few of her delicious honey buns and sweet milk would go quite perfectly with it. So I grabbed the jug, but wouldn't ye know it? Agnes spotted me. She shouted at me to bring her back the jug, but at that point, it was rather a fun game to run from her, so I gave her a merry chase around the table. By that time, my father heard the commotion and came thundering into the kitchen. Well, my arse was still smarting from the mischief I'd done the day before, so I ran out of the back door, forgetting about the snow. I slipped and dropped the jug of sweet milk into the snow, my face falling right into it. I lapped up the snow like a dog lapping a bone, all while my father smacked my wayward rear."

Guinevere laughed so hard, she snorted, and that only made Brody laugh all the harder.

"Agnes watched the whole episode with keen interest. Wouldn't ye know it, that night after supper, the whole of the castle was served sweet snow milk."

"That is truly a remarkable and amusing story."

Brody sat back in his chair, staring at his wife with appreciation. Saints, but she was a beauty. "Tell me a story, wife."

"What kind of story? I didn't create any delicious recipes."

Brody chuckled and pointed his spoon at her. "That ye know of. Tell me something ye did as a child that got ye into trouble, and now looking back on it, ye laugh."

She snickered. "Well, 'tis actually ironic considering the fiasco with our chamber door here." Guinevere set her empty cup down on the table beside her chair. "My sisters and I, we had no brothers, and so my father was often telling us stories of his exploits and how to protect ourselves. We decided one day to play 'storm the castle'. In the woods, we found the thickest branches we could carry, dragged them right up to the door of our keep and proceeded to bang them against the wood, shouting to be let in, that the castle was under siege and we were all going to die. The entire castle was in an uproar, thinking something terrible had happened. Guards came running, women hid, and we destroyed the door so thoroughly, my father wouldn't let us out of our nursery for a week. Porridge and milk were all the sustenance we were allowed. My mother forced us to leave the room when father told stories of his exploits for at least a year after that."

Brody laughed so hard his head fell back and tears came to his eyes. "Did ye ever storm the castle again?" he asked.

"Nay, but we did plenty of other things to cause mischief. And what of you? Any other delicious recipes result from your tormenting the cook?"

"Nay, but I did see her spill plenty of things in the snow and taste them afterward."

They laughed again, only to be interrupted by Noah entering the great hall. Both of them looked to see if Elinor followed as she did most mornings, but she was not beside him.

"Marischal." Noah held a missive in his hand.

Guinevere glanced between the both of them nervously. "I'll take our cups back to the kitchen."

She stood to leave, but Brody stayed her. "Dinna leave. Ye're my wife. Ye've as much right to the information contained in any missive."

Guinevere bit her lip and looked anxious, as though she wasn't quite certain of her place in this new world.

"Stay," he said gently. "For me."

Guinevere nodded, setting the two cups back down and folding her hands in front of her.

"Arrived just now, I saw the messenger ride up."

Brody took the scroll. "Wallace's seal." He broke the wax and unrolled the parchment.

Marischal Keith,

By the time this letter reaches ye, we'll be across the border and back in Scotland once more, headed for Selkirk where I've been summoned by de Brus. I'll be knighted, and the men will return home for a time to be with their families and protect their properties.

The English appear to be buckling down for the winter as well, but that does not mean we will stop.

I was surprised to receive your news regarding Arundel, but pleased, as well. Given the truth of the French's treachery, it is good to see more men on our side than running to Longshanks' deep coffers.

I've sent your men back to East Lothian, and will summon you again when the time comes to regroup.

One last thing, and this is for Noah. I regret to be the bearer of bad news, but it is now evident that Chief Oliphant is an Edward supporter. A continued alliance with the Oliphant's daughter would be seen as treason.

W.W.

Brody looked up from the missive to find two expectant pairs of eyes boring into his.

"Wallace has returned to Scotland. He's going to be knighted by de Brus."

"That is good news and well deserved," Noah said.

"He's sent the men home to regroup and will call upon us when needed."

"When does he say that might be?" Guinevere asked, biting her lip. Though she tried to hide it, he could see the deep worry in her eyes.

Brody took her hand in his, bringing it to his lips to kiss her knuckles. "Not for months I expect."

"Then I won't have to worry about your toes freezing just yet?" She was trying to make light of the situation, but there was a nervous edge to her voice.

"Or any other part." Brody decided to make light of it, too, at least to distract her from her worry. It was too soon after her ordeal for her to fear whether he'd leave or not.

She blushed and Noah shifted uncomfortably. Brody's grin widened.

"If ye'll excuse me," his cousin murmured.

"Wait, there was something else, Noah." Brody took a deep breath, about to break the bad news. Though he wondered just how bad it would be. "It appears that Oliphant has sided with Edward."

"What?" Noah's face constricted in anger. "Traitor!"

"Aye. It means ye canna marry his daughter." Brody shook his head in mock disappointment. Aye, he'd wanted the alliance, but he also knew what misery it would be for Noah, now that it appeared he'd found love elsewhere. What had come over him? He never would have cared what the heart wanted before now. "We'll not be associated with traitors."

"Nay, of course not." Noah dragged in a breath. "I understand." Instead of looking upset, however, he simply looked relived.

And Brody had a good idea of why, but he wanted to tease his cousin a little. "I've an idea for another clan alliance, however, so we needn't worry overly much about it. The Grants, perhaps."

Noah looked like he was going to be sick to his stomach.

"They've a daughter or two who've yet to wed," Brody continued. "Or maybe even the MacDougals. That bastard's got at least a dozen daughters."

Noah cleared his throat. "Let us not worry over that now. We'll talk later." And then he was backing out of the great hall slowly, like a dog trying to steal away without his master taking notice of it.

"Oh, come now, we should discuss it now. A spring wedding!" Brody called jovially.

Noah all but ran from the room with Brody laughing behind him.

"You tease him," Guinevere said, leaning against his side.

"Of course. I think he's got another in his mind."

She nodded, sliding her arms around his waist and looking up at him. "And I think she's quite besotted with him, even if she's yet to admit it."

"And what about ye?" Brody stroked her cheek, slid his fingers through her hair. "Are ye besotted?"

Guinevere frowned. "I should be, but…"

Brody's stomach did a flip and then she laughed.

"Even you can be teased," she murmured, lifting up on her tiptoes to kiss him on the lips. "Always so strong and confident, you are. Someone has to take you in hand without Agnes or your father here to do it."

"Och, lass, ye're offering to be the one?"

"Aye. I'd be more than happy."

Brody slid his lips over hers, breathing in the sweet vanilla and honey of their treat. "What sort of chastisement did ye have in mind?"

She giggled and pressed her breasts against him, running her hands up and down his spine. His body reacted immediately, growing hot and hard. If they weren't in the great hall, he would have dragged her down to the rushes right then and there.

"We'll have to go to our chamber, for I'd not want anyone to witness your shame." Her voice was filled with taunting mirth.

"Och. Ye slay me." He swept her up into his arms and headed for the stairs, eager for whatever delicious torment she had in store.

Chapter Twenty-Three

"Here are three more." Elinor handed Guinevere the small wool blankets she'd been gathering for the children in the surrounding villages.

"We've about thirty now." Placing her hands on her hips she examined the two overflowing baskets. "'Tis not enough, but a good start at least."

"They will be happy you thought of them."

"'Tis the least I could do."

Guinevere had done this very same thing the year before, though she'd not been able to gather as many blankets. Most of them she'd made from scrap pieces of wool or plaids that were falling apart. She cut out the good pieces and sewed them together.

"What's this?" Brody strolled into their room a surprised look on his face. "Ye've got your mantle on. Where are ye going?" He almost looked hurt that he'd not been included.

Guinevere approached her husband wrapping her arms around his waist and reaching up to give him a quick kiss. "To deliver blankets to the children."

"Alone?" There was thunder in his gaze and he'd nearly shouted the word.

Guinevere frowned. "Of course not. Elinor is coming with me. And Noah agreed to be our escort."

Brody looked hurt, giving her a small pout. "Ye didna ask me."

"Oh." Guinevere frowned, stroked her fingers over his brow. "I'm sorry. I thought you'd be busy with my father. As a matter of fact, I didn't expect to see you for some time. It's only just after noon."

He'd been holed up in his library for two days with her father, only coming out at night to make love and sleep. She'd not realized until he showed her, just how many holdings he had, and there were many plans that needed to be made for her father who would take over as constable in the north at Caithness.

Brody shook his head. "We're mostly done. I came to see if ye wanted to eat the nooning with me."

She bit her lip. "I already ate..." Lord, but she felt terrible. "I—"

Brody gave her quick kiss on the lips. "Dinna fash. Ye're right, I have been working nonstop the last two days. I will ask Cook to pack me something I can eat while we're out."

"You want to come?" She was surprised and excited. Brody had yet to make any rounds of the village, and it would be so great to do it with him for the first time.

"Aye." He bent to a basket and plucked up one of the blankets. "These are wonderful. What made ye think of it?"

"My first winter here was misery. I was so cold, and all I could think about were the children. How they must also be cold. Men were tossing holy blankets on the fire, saying they weren't worth mending. Well, I thought they were, so my ladies and I, we took the rest and reshaped them for children."

"Ye have a heart of gold, ye know that, *iasg beag*?"

Guinevere rolled her eyes. "I don't know about a heart of gold, or that I simply don't want the little imps to freeze."

He grinned and refolded the blanket, settling it back in the basket. "Either way, I'm certain they love ye for it."

"I'd do it even if they didn't."

"And that is why they love ye—and a perfect example of your golden heart."

Guinevere peeked out the window to see the sky was full white once more. "We'd best go. Snow is bound to start falling soon and I'd hate for us to get stuck in it."

"Aye." Brody stacked the two baskets and lifted them easily.

Guinevere admired his strength. It took her and Elinor sharing the load of each basket to get them down the stairs. "Are you certain you can do both?"

Brody chuckled and to prove his point, lifted his arms straight up in the air so both heavy baskets were over his head.

Guinevere tickled his ribs. "All right, you've made your point."

"Love, I toss cabers for fun. If I can toss a tree, I can carry a couple baskets of blankets."

Now that was a sight she'd like to see.

"Ladies first," Brody said, nodding toward the door.

Mantle's pulled tight and muffs covering their hands, Guinevere and Elinor made their way down the stairs and out to the bailey where Noah already had four horses waiting.

"How did ye know?" Brody asked.

"Saw ye come out of the library and head up the stairs. Also, thought ye might want something to eat seeing as how ye've barely done so in two days." Noah held up a small linen sack. "Nothing special, but Cook assured me ye'd be pleased."

"My thanks."

They strapped the baskets onto the horses and then Brody helped Guinevere to mount, his hands stroking with taunting intent over her rear. She raised her brow in mock outrage, but he only chuckled and pinched her teasingly.

With a glance toward Elinor and Noah, she saw that he, too, helped her to mount. The attraction and friendship between the two of them was growing. So much so, Guinevere was certain a proposal would be made soon—and if it wasn't, she and Brody might have to insist on it.

They rode their horses through the gate, taking the path slow as the ground was still covered in snow from the previous falling. Brody ate with gusto the chicken and scones in the sack, offering bites to Guinevere, but she declined. She liked to watch him eat, the passion he put into it was almost as much as when they made love.

About half an hour later, limbs frigid, they arrived in the quiet village. Smoke curled from makeshift chimneys in the

257

various wattle and daub crofts. About two dozen crofts were built across from one another in a line, fairly close together, creating a narrow street. At the head was a small parish, and a few workshops, and a well. Behind each croft, dwellers each had several acres of land they could plant, and space to raise animals.

Part of their crops went to the castle, some to market and the rest for themselves. With winter, most of the crofters would continue to care for their animals, prepare their seeds, get to repairs they'd not yet done when weather permitted, and catch up on sleep if they were able. A lot of children were conceived in the winter.

That thought had Guinevere touching her own belly, wondering if there would soon be a child growing in her womb—or if there was already.

Some children played outside, while fathers worked to clear their roofs of heavy pockets of snow. Dogs romped. 'Twas rather inviting.

"The laird! The lady!" shouted a small child rushing into his croft.

Several men and women came out of their doors and bowed or curtsied, welcoming them into the small village. Those who'd been on their roofs, climbed down to greet them.

"We've brought blankets for your children, if they are in need," Guinevere said.

"Thank ye, mistress." Several mothers spoke their gratitude and stepped forward to accept the blankets. "Ye're welcome to come in and have a bite. We've a warm pottage over the fire."

Politeness bade them accept and they were invited into the first house, while several others hurried home to grab bread, cheese, dried fruit or ale. They all wanted to share, to show their thanks.

The four of them accepted, though they didn't consume much, as the crofters needed their fare more.

"My lady, we have built a snow lady that looks like ye! Come see! Come see!" Several children burst into the croft, cheeks red from cold and excitement.

Guinevere smiled and stood. Brody and Noah had been in an intense conversation with the lead crofter of the town, and when they both stood to join her, she waved them back down. "I'll be right back."

Outside, she delighted in the angular and round snow creature. They'd put strands of hay on the head to form her golden locks, and rocks for the eyes, nose and mouth.

"Ma said we couldn't use the carrots and apples like I wanted to," one little boy pouted.

"'Tis all right, I quite love it!" Guinevere hugged them each, ruffling their hair.

Their little hands were red and purple from cold. She'd need to make them some gloves, little woolen ones with the small scraps she couldn't use for making blankets.

"My lady." A young girl came forward, eyes wide with concern. "The woman said to give you this."

From behind her back she pulled a crude doll, the head pulled off and sewn to the belly. Guinevere startled. The sight of the headless doll was a gruesome shock, and a threatening message at that. Guinevere reached for the doll if only to relieve the child of its hideousness. She took a step back and looked off into the direction the child had come from to find whoever the woman was, but the street was empty.

"Who?" she asked. "Who gave you this?"

The little girl shrugged. "I've never seen her before. She was behind the parish."

Clutching the doll, Guinevere marched as quickly as she could through six inches of snow, toward the parish. The headless doll was an obvious threat. But who would want to harm her? Her instinct screamed Mrs. Donald. But she'd been exiled. Was it possible she'd come back to Dunnottar? And if she had, who would have harbored the bitter old woman?

The closer she got, the more the sounds from the first village house where they all gathered lessened, until she reached complete quiet. She took the steps carefully up to the door of the small kirk, reaching for the handle and opening it. Inside was quiet, bare. Her footsteps echoed just as loudly as her heart pounded.

"Hello?" she called.

With her grip on the doll in one hand, she fingered the dagger she wore at her hip, ready to yank it free should someone leap out at her.

There was no answer to her call, only the deafening silence that made her stomach flip. Every nerve had leapt to attention, the hair on the back of her neck prickling, her throat dry.

Benches were lined up on either side, six deep, and the altar at the front stood empty. She passed each one, staring beneath them as though a demon might leap from beneath.

A few brave priests had remained behind after de Ros had come, and she thought she had met the one who resided in this small village before, but now she questioned that. It was empty, cold and barren in the kirk.

She walked to the back, peeking out a small window, when the door closed loudly behind her.

Guinevere jumped and turned around.

Standing by the door was Mrs. Donald.

She was alone and her face was filled with murderous intent. Her clothes were threadbare and she looked frailer than before. More weathered. Haggard. Like an old witch that haunted the forests searching for children to eat for supper.

"What are you doing here?" Guinevere asked.

"I've more a right to be here than ye do." The sneer on the older woman's visage completely puckered her face, her lip coming near to her nose and her brows so furrowed they touched.

"As a matter of fact, you do not." Guinevere straightened, having practiced so many times in her head just how she would conduct herself if she was ever faced with this woman again. "Your laird banished you. An act of mercy."

"He might as well have sentenced me to death." Her voice was brittle, no longer filled with as much strength as she'd had when she was at the castle.

"And why is that? You're a decent cook, when you try. And if all else fails, you could earn a penny at a local tavern serving slop to drunken fools."

Mrs. Donald advanced a few slow paces, a noticeable limp on her left side. "Slop is no less than what ye deserve, ye *Sassenach* rubbish."

Guinevere breathed out a sigh filled with pity. "Why do you hate me so much, when I've only ever tried to be peaceful?"

"Peace does not run in your blood."

She shook her head. "You know not what runs in my blood."

"Vicious. Vile. Devil's spawn." With each word Mrs. Donald stabbed her finger toward her.

Guinevere bristled. She'd been trying hard to remain calm. To allow the older woman to say her piece, but it appeared she would only continue to spew venom.

"I will give you a chance to run, Mrs. Donald. A chance to hide, before I tell my husband that you're here. Another chance to see that I am not what you think."

Mrs. Donald laughed. "I'll not give ye the same, bitch. I've the four men ye had banished all outside as well. We've got ye surrounded. And we're starving. We're cold. So, 'tis not likely they'll be kind when they shred ye to pieces."

Guinevere pressed her lips together, swallowing hard. She glanced out the window to see that, indeed, there were four men outside, each of them brandishing a sword, and looking just as haggard as the old cook.

"I won't be able to save you all a second time."

Mrs. Donald laughed. "We're not interested in saving. Only vengeance."

"Who hurt you?" Guinevere asked. "Because it wasn't me."

"Johanna and Laird Keith were not the only ones murdered by your kind that day," Mrs. Donald seethed. "They took my boy. They took my two granddaughters. All I had left in the world."

"But I didn't. You cannot hold every Englishman accountable."

"And why not?"

"Should I hate every Scot because one cook sold me for a bag of silver to my enemy?"

Mrs. Donald grunted.

Outside, the men shouted and started advancing toward someone.

Brody! He and Noah were alone against four armed men. Three of them warriors trained by Brody himself. He'd not allow the crofters to fight for him out of pride and so he planned to take them on himself. She could see it in the determined set of his jaw through the small window. Even as she took note of that, she realized that the four miserable warriors were no match for two seasoned, well fed ones.

"They will die," Guinevere said. "And then so will you."

Mrs. Donald spat.

"You just defiled the church." Guinevere frowned. "Surrender now. You have lost."

"Ye only hope that I've lost."

Guinevere shook her head and looked on the woman with pity. "'Tis a certainty."

Swords clanged outside the kirk, mingled with shouts. She could hear Brody calling for her.

"I'm here! I'm all right!" she called back, not sure if he could hear her.

"Ye'll not be fine if I've anything to say." And then Mrs. Donald ran toward her, a knife brandished in her gnarled hand.

CHAPTER TWENTY-FOUR

When a person with crazed eyes ran at another, weapon drawn and death the only thing on their maddened mind, instincts bade one to either flee or fight.

Guinevere was ready to fight.

That was what Brody would do. And she was Brody's wife. She was mistress to a powerful clan. Daughter to a brave leader. She had the strength. She would fight to win. No longer would she be a victim.

The woman flying at her like a banshee straight from the very depths of Hell, was one who'd tormented her for months on end with foul food, rude comments, and then, of course, the pinnacle of her torment, the witch had sold her to an enemy who fully planned to rape and murder her.

Not to mention that Guinevere's hair had not fully grown back where it had needed to be cut low so the healer could stitch her back together.

She wrenched the dagger from its sheath and planted her feet on the floor. But the closer Mrs. Donald drew, she knew it would not be easy to simply block the blow herself.

At the last second, she ducked to the right, sticking her foot out and tripping the older woman, who went flying toward the altar. She landed with a hard thud and a guttural bellow.

Guinevere screamed, instinct forcing her to drop by the woman's side to check on her. She'd knelt and placed her hand on the woman's bony back before she'd even had a chance to think that was a bad idea.

Mrs. Donald growled like a feral animal, rolling over to show her blade lodged in her chest. She'd stabbed herself when she'd fallen—nay, when Guinevere had tripped her. Blood pooled dark on her filthy garments.

"Bitch," the crone managed to ground out, a small trickle of blood at the corner of her lip.

"You didn't have to die," Guinevere said, tears coming to her eyes, her voice filled with anguish. She'd never killed anyone before. "You just needed to leave."

"Same difference," Mrs. Donald croaked.

Mrs. Donald clutched the hilt of her dagger, and when Guinevere thought she would try to pull it out, she sank it deeper, groaning at the pain.

The door to the kirk burst open behind them, revealing Brody, blood splattered on his cloak, and Noah right behind him. They took in the sight of Mrs. Donald's death mask.

"She fell," Guinevere explained.

265

"Then she is lucky, for I would have run her through," Brody said. The scowl on his face was full of pain, regret and anger. "'Tis the second time I've failed ye."

Guinevere climbed to her feet and hurried toward her husband, throwing herself in his arms. "Nay. You didn't. You cannot be here all the time. I have to learn to take care of myself. I should."

"Och, lass, but ye shouldna have to, though ye showed how brave ye are." He kissed her deeply, clutching her to him so hard she could barely breathe. "I need to get ye home. I need to lock us both in our chamber and take ye into my arms."

"Please, Brody. Right now." She buried her face in his chest. "I love you, so much."

"*Tha gaol agam ort, iasg beag.*"

Three months later

The first thistle of spring bloomed on the very day the final piece was put on the kirk. Spring had finally arrived and with it, so many wonderful things.

Guinevere's sisters sat at the trestle table with their mother and father. Across from them was Maire and Brody's mother.

Cook had prepared a feast fit for a king, which was good because de Brus and Wallace had arrived two days before to wish the newlyweds well and proclaimed that a tournament was long overdue.

Missives were sent out to the neighboring clans and now hundreds of men pooled in their bailey awaiting the games. There would be a rock climbing contest. A caber toss. A stone throwing contest. And when the men had thoroughly exhausted their bodies there would be a battle of wits—chess and knucklebones. Much feasting and dancing.

There was a magic in the air that Dunnottar had long missed, and that brought a constant smile to Guinevere's lips.

"Are ye ready to see your husband lose to a greater warrior?" Wallace asked, a teasing glint in his eyes, as they sat feasting at the table.

Guinevere laughed. She patted Brody on his thick, muscular leg. "Aye, I have heard his cousin, Noah, is very talented."

Wallace's eyes widened and then he burst into a deep, rumbling laugh. "Ye're a witty one."

Guinevere winked, surprised to see that Wallace blushed slightly.

"Are ye ready?" Brody puffed his chest, taking a mighty bite from a turkey leg. "A tournament to outrank all others."

"A wager!" The way Wallace said it made it seem as though the men had done this many times before.

"Aye! Your sword." Brody grinned and nodded toward the claymore strapped at his leader's back.

"A kiss from your wife."

"Prepare to say goodbye to your sword." Brody tossed his turkey leg at Wallace, who caught it in mid-air and took a huge bite.

"Prepare for your wife to fall in love with me," Wallace said, laughing around a mouth full of meat.

Guinevere was laughing so hard tears came to her eyes.

Soon, they headed in a long line to the fields that had been set up in record time. Tents were erected for the ladies to sit beneath as they watched the men, complete with braziers and blankets since the weather was still cool. Meat roasted on open pits and there was enough ale and wine to make it flow like a fountain.

The men were primed for the challenges they would face, shouting and laughing and raising their fists. Guinevere had never seen anything like it. And Brody, he couldn't stop grinning—but that was for an entirely different matter.

She'd woken him up that morning, placing his hand on the small swell of her belly. "Our baby," she'd whispered.

"A bairn? Truly?" His eyes had lit up, his smile spread so wide, she was certain his face might crack, and it hadn't faltered yet.

They were going to have a baby. A child they could feed snow milk to in the winter, a child they could play knucklebones with and a child whose antics were likely to drive them just as mad as they'd driven their own parents.

A herald bounded into the center of the field, shouting for the attention of the warriors as well as the spectators. Crofters had come from miles away to watch, setting up tents in the fields, as the games were likely to go on for at least a few days followed by several days of celebrating before their other duties began in earnest requiring them to work from dawn to dusk with little break between.

"I'm so pleased that Brody met and married ye," Maire said, coming to sit beside Guinevere. "I've never seen him so happy. And after what happened… Well, we were all certain he'd be the laird of dread for the rest of his days."

Guinevere smiled and patted Maire's hand. "He blames himself for what happened still, but knowing that he was able to save me, to rid the earth of Gray, he's started to heal."

"And ye? Are ye happy?"

"Very. I never thought I would say it. Especially not here, in Scotland, but I have made a home here. I have made friends. I have fallen in love." She pressed her hand to her belly. "We have started a family."

Maire squealed, drawing the attention of every other female in the tent, who fawned over Guinevere.

But then the herald announced the men would be throwing cabers and Guinevere's eyes were riveted on the pure strength of the warrior lifting the tree trunks two or three times their height, straight up into the air and flinging them. She could barely lift a stone and here they were tossing cabers.

'Twas truly astonishing.

Brody's went the furthest in the first round, but he lost to Noah in the second. Not to be beat, Wallace gave them all a run for their coin when his landed three feet from where Brody's had lain in round one. But Brody wasn't about to let Wallace kiss her, and so he challenged them again, throwing it nearly five feet from where he had before—beating Wallace by two feet. There was a lot to say when it came to jealous strength. Guinevere and all the ladies in the tent giggled over the men's competitive nature.

The games drew to a halt so they could all feast. Brody tugged her into his arms and she made a grand gesture of touching his muscles and cooing over his strength. He swung her up in a circle, round and round, ending in a kiss that had what sounded like everyone in the land cheering.

When they returned to the games, they threw large stones, the size of a man's head, and then smaller ones, at targets. They tested themselves with a bow and then on horseback with a quintain.

More feasting ensued and Guinevere fell asleep in her chair, waking to Brody placing her in bed.

"I love ye," he said, kissing her. "Ye've made me a better man. A whole man."

Guinevere stroked the side of his stubbled face. "We complete each other. I was lost before you found me. Living a life without a path and filled with unhappiness."

"Ye seemed verra determined when I found ye running on the beach, seemed ye knew the path there," he teased.

She laughed. "Living was perhaps the only thing I knew for certain I wanted."

"I'm glad ye decided to live your life with me."

She stroked the side of his face. "I'm glad you offered."

"I couldn't have left ye. The moment ye stood up to me in your chamber, I was mesmerized. And by the time I found ye on the beach, I was all but in love."

Guinevere laughed and tugged him closer. "It might have been the first time I ever stood up for myself. You showed me I could be strong."

Brody cupped her cheek, gazing into her eyes. "And now this." His fingers trailed over her collarbone, between her breasts down to her belly.

"A miracle," she whispered, leaning up to capture his lips with her own. She savored the woodsy, masculine scent of him, the fragrance of the outdoors still clinging to him. He tasted of honey and rosemary, the aftereffects of the sweet cake Cook had made.

Brody deepened their kiss, gathering her against him. He stroked her back, deftly divesting her and himself of their clothes. Passion consumed them both, and though they'd only been married a few short months, both of them knew just how to touch, tease and kiss to drive the other one wild.

With nothing but a haze of wonder, Brody consumed her. He drove into her, wrapping her legs up around his hips, and when she was on the brink of climax, he stilled, tormenting her all the more. Rolling to his back, he pulled her over him, a position she knew well she could take the lead. Fingers threaded together over his head, she kissed him as she set the pace.

Brody groaned, no longer able to stall their delicious finish, and Guinevere took him all the way to the end—an end that would only lead, yet once more, to another beginning. For they were never truly finished, only waiting, and anticipating the very next time they could be together.

"I love you, savage."

"*Tha gaol agam ort, iasg beag.*"

THE END

If you enjoyed **STOLEN BY THE LAIRD***, please spread the word by leaving a review on the site where you purchased your copy, or a reader site such as Goodreads or Shelfari! I love to hear from readers, too, so drop me a line at* <u>authorelizaknight@gmail.com</u> *OR visit me on Facebook:* <u>https://www.facebook.com/elizaknightauthor</u>. I'm also on Twitter: @ElizaKnight. If you'd like to receive my occasional newsletter, please sign up at <u>www.elizaknight.com.</u> *Many thanks!*

ABOUT THE AUTHOR

Eliza Knight is an award-winning and *USA Today* bestselling indie author of sizzling historical romance and erotic romance. Under the name E. Knight, she pens rip-your-heart-out historical fiction. While not reading, writing or researching for her latest book, she chases after her three children. In her spare time (if there is such a thing…) she likes daydreaming, wine-tasting, traveling, hiking, staring at the stars, watching movies, shopping and visiting with family and friends. She lives atop a small mountain with her own knight in shining armor, three princesses and two very naughty puppies. Visit Eliza at http://www.elizaknight.com or her historical blog History Undressed: www.historyundressed.com

More Books by Eliza Knight

The Conquered Bride Series
Conquered by the Highlander
Seduced by the Laird
Taken by the Highlander (Captured by a Celtic Warrior anthology)
Claimed by the Warrior
Stolen by the Laird

Coming soon…
Protected by the Laird (Enchanted by the Highlander anthology)
Laird of Shadows (Once Upon a Haunted Castle anthology)

The Stolen Bride Series
The Highlander's Temptation
The Highlander's Reward
The Highlander's Conquest
The Highlander's Lady
The Highlander's Warrior Bride
The Highlander's Triumph
The Highlander's Sin
Wild Highland Mistletoe—a Stolen Bride winter novella
The Highlander's Charm
A Kilted Christmas Wish – a contemporary Holiday spin-off

The Thistles and Roses Series
Eternally Bound
Promise of a Knight

Coming soon…
Breath from the Sea (Ever My Love Collection)

Under the name E. Knight

Tales From the Tudor Court
My Lady Viper
Prisoner of the Queen

Ancient Historical Fiction
A Day of Fire: a novel of Pompeii
A Year of Ravens: a novel of Boudica's Rebellion

Made in the USA
San Bernardino, CA
14 July 2016